CHARLIE'S KEY

ROB MILLS

ORCA BOOK PUBLISHERS

Library and Archives Canada Cataloguing in Publication

Mills, Rob, 1961-
Charlie's key / Rob Mills.

Issued also in electronic formats.
ISBN 978-1-55469-872-1

I. Title.
PS8626.I4566C43 2011   JC813'.6   C2011-903508-1

First published in the United States, 2011
Library of Congress Control Number: 2011907484

Summary: A young orphan struggles to unlock the significance
of an old key left by his dying father.

*Orca Book Publishers is dedicated to preserving the environment and has printed
this book on paper certified by the Forest Stewardship Council.*®

Orca Book Publishers gratefully acknowledges the support for its publishing
programs provided by the following agencies: the Government of Canada through
the Canada Book Fund and the Canada Council for the Arts, and the Province of
British Columbia through the BC Arts Council and the Book Publishing Tax Credit.

Design by Teresa Bubela
Cover photography by Michael Richard Crotty
Author photo by Miranda Studios

ORCA BOOK PUBLISHERS   ORCA BOOK PUBLISHERS
PO Box 5626, Stn. B   PO Box 468
Victoria, BC Canada   Custer, WA USA
V8R 6S4   98240-0468

www.orcabook.com
Printed and bound in Canada.

14   13   12   11   •   4   3   2   1

For Kelly and Hannah,
and for my first reader, Lydia,
who looked in the pot each day after school.

ONE

My dad never saw what killed him—leastways, that's what the cops said. Not that they ever said it to my face. I heard them talking when I was lying in the hospital bed. When they figured I was still knocked out. In fact it's the first thing I can remember after the accident—those cops talking. One minute I'm in the backseat of the car, my forehead cool against the window, watching the broken yellow lines flash past. The next, there's those two cops talking in the hallway, yanking me up outta somewhere gray and soft.

"Never seen what he hit," says one.

"Never do," says the other. "Not at night. Just come outta the woods and *bang*—you're on top of 'em."

"Come through the windshield—nearly tore him in half—then sailed right over the kid sleeping in the back."

"Still alive?"

"The kid?"

"No, the dad."

"Barely. Hasn't said a word, hasn't opened his eyes. Nothing."

"Not good."

The one cop didn't say anything to that, so I figured he musta just shook his head.

"Next of kin?" one asked the other.

"Don't know. Dad can't tell us, kid is still unconscious, nothing in the car."

"Nothing?"

"Nope. No papers, no permit, no insurance."

"Just moose."

They laugh at that. Which is when I decide to say something. Or try to say something. Only nothing comes out except a moan—loud enough, though, for them cops to hear. I open my eyes but can't see much—just shadows. But I can hear plenty.

"Doc," one of the cops yells. "Doc—kid's awake."

The shadows move toward me, hands on my head and my wrist; then it all goes blank, till there's a new voice calling out, "Son, son."

It could be my dad, so I work hard to open my eyes. But it's not my dad. It's some doctor, all blurry white coat and gold glasses. He's leaning over me with his face as big and white as the sun up in the summer sky when you lie on the grass looking up. Except you can't look at the sun for a long time, 'cause it'll burn the retinas right outta your head in about two seconds. I blink a few times, and slowly my head starts to clear.

I can tell the little beep I hear is coming from a machine by my head, and I can smell the nurse's shampoo when she bends close to me to read something on it. Then I can see the doctor's got little bumps of black on his chin, like he hasn't shaved in a couple of days. And I can tell what he's saying.

"Son," he says, "you've been in an accident. You've been unconscious for a couple of hours. Do you understand?"

I start to nod but stop real quick since it makes me feel like I got kicked in the back of my head.

"You're going to be okay," he says, "but the other person in the car, the driver..."

"My dad."

"Your dad. He's been injured. Badly. Would you like to see him?"

I nod again, even though I know it'll hurt.

"Okay," says the doctor. He nods to a nurse and she goes off to the hall, coming back a sec later with a wheelchair.

"Before we go up," the doctor says, "we'd like to call your mom. Can you tell me her name? Give me her phone number?"

"I don't got a mom."

The doctor looks at the cops, then back to me. "A sister or brother or a grandma?"

"It's just me and my dad."

One of the cops starts to say something, but the other one gives him a jab. Then it's just that monitor beeping and the nurse poking at some stuff till the doctor talks again.

"Okay," he says. "So let's take you up to see your dad. What's your name?"

One of the cops pulls a notepad outta his shirt pocket.

"Charlie," I say. "Charlie Sykes."

"Sykes?" says the cop. He's looking at his buddy, then at me. "Sykes?" he says again, his eyebrows halfway up his forehead.

"All right," the doctor says to them, angry, like he's breaking up a fight at recess. He turns back to me.

"Okay, Charlie. And what's your father's name?"

"Michael," I say, which gets the cop yapping again, louder this time.

"Jesus," the cop says. "Mikey Sykes."

"Enough," says the doctor, turning round to look at the cops. "You'll have to be quiet or I'll ask you to leave."

One cop—older, fatter—shakes his head. "Ask away, Doc, but we're staying."

The doctor gets ready to say something else, but the cop holds up a hand and waves it in his face.

"We," he says, slow and quiet, still waving his fat fingers. "Are. Staying."

The doctor lets out a sigh.

"All right," he says. Then he and the nurse leave the room. A couple a minutes later they're back, with the nurse bending close to help me into the chair. She's soft and smells good, and it's nice, that feeling, when she puts her arms around me to help me into the seat—nice and so warm that I get a bit cold and shivery when she lets go.

"Okay, Charlie," she says, getting behind me to push the chair. "Let's go see your dad."

We head down a hallway to the elevator, the cops right behind us. The doors rattle open and I get pushed in first, a couple of old folks moving back to make room for me. The doctor comes aboard behind the nurse and turns to the cops as soon as he's in. He holds up his hand and waves his fingers right in the fat cop's face.

"Get the next one," he says.

The cop puts his arm between the doors when they start to close—the doors are ugly green and chipped from where stuff has banged into them—but he yanks it out just before they shut, which I don't blame him for doing, 'cause I'd a pulled my hand outta there too. We go up two floors and the cops are there waiting when the doors open, the fat one bent over, puffing.

"We're coming with you," his partner says, while the fat guy's head bobs up and down, his red chins bouncing off his blue shirt. The doctor doesn't say anything, just heads through a door marked ICU, with me and the nurse and the cops all following along. I thought maybe my dad would be in a quiet room, a dark room, since he was hurt so bad, but this room is all lit up and full of noise and machines. We stop at the end of a bed that's covered with electric cords and plastic tubes. It stinks in here, like that corner in the boys' locker room where Randy Simms peed after Mr. Connors yelled at him for doing sit-ups wrong. I guess it must stink like that in here all the time, 'cause no one else wrinkles their nose or anything. Instead, the doctor bends down to talk to me. His knee makes a pop when he squats.

"Charlie," he says, "you and your dad…your car hit a moose on the highway. It did a lot of damage, and your dad is in a coma. But he might be able to hear. So you could talk to him. Do you want to do that?"

But I'm not listening to the doctor; I'm more just looking at the guy in the bed, thinking there must be a mistake.

"That's my dad?" I ask after a minute. "'Cause that doesn't look like my dad."

It's true. It doesn't. My dad has wavy black hair that curls on the sides and the sorta face that a tough guy on TV might have—where you can see his jaw muscles bulge out when he gets angry. The guy in this bed has got his head shaved, and his face is all soft and puffy. There's a tube coming out his mouth. He looks like a sick Pillsbury Dough Boy, not like my dad. No way.

"This is your dad," says the doctor. He's looking between me and the nurse. Up to her, down to me.

"Charlie," he says, up to the nurse, down to me, "he's very sick. And you should try and talk to him. C'mon."

He holds out his hand and I take it, which even right then I think is funny, 'cause I've only ever held my dad's hand before, and it's been a long time since I did that—not since I was little and I almost ran out into the street outside the clinic in Edmonton, before my dad grabbed my arm and yanked me back.

"Here," the doctor says. "Sit beside him, up here on the bed. It's okay."

Now I see maybe it is my dad. He's got that scar on his chin, and his nose has that bump where it got broke.

I look for his watch—the one we said could come from me at Christmas—but it's not there.

"He has a watch," I say.

"We had to take it off," says the doctor. "Because of the edema."

"The swelling," says the nurse. "That's making him puffy. You'll get it back…"

She doesn't finish what she's saying, but I guess what it is, and that's the first time I feel myself getting soft inside, feel stuff coming up to my eyes and that soft sizzling in my nose. And right then the doctor and the nurse and the cops and the noise all kinda disappear and it's just me and my dad, and it is my dad, I see now. There's that scar, and the white hair poking straight up in his eyebrow, and a dent where his watch was. I can feel it when I put my hand on his.

"Dad," I say, leaning down close to whisper to him, even though it hurts my head to bend over. "Dad, it's me. Charlie."

He doesn't say anything. I knew he wouldn't, but he might have. Maybe. But he doesn't. Just lays there, still, warm. Then I feel his hand twitch and twitch again. I put both my hands around his. And then, just a tiny bit, it opens. Then a bit more, and I feel something drop out of it, small, hard, hot in my palm. A key. I can tell without even looking.

And as soon as I feel it, all the noise and voices and other people in the room come flooding back—the *beep* and *swish-schonk* of the machine by my dad's bed. And especially the looks on the faces of those two cops, all pinched and pointy and looking right at me and my dad. Something about how they're looking at me makes me keep my mouth shut, makes me clamp down on that key and decide, right then, not to say a word about it. I don't know what it's for or what it opens, but I know I'm going to keep it. I'm not going to give anybody a chance to take it away, like they took away his watch, and then have to depend on them to give it back. Back to me, a kid without a mom. Or a dad.

Because I know, as soon as it happens. Some buzzer goes off, and the doctor all of a sudden pulls me off the bed and puts me back in the wheelchair, and the nurse pushes me outta the room. But I already know: my dad is gone and I'm alone. I knew it as soon as that key hit my hand.

TWO

I sleep a lot the next day, or I think I do—I can't remember much, except that every time I wake up, that fat cop is sitting in the hallway outside my room. He's mostly outta sight, but whenever I look that way, I can see the tips of his boots and his gut and his hat.

"Why's he sitting there?" I ask the nurse, but she just smiles and tells me not to worry—he's just making sure I'm okay. Which doesn't make me feel any more okay. Why would I need a cop sitting outside my door? Maybe somebody is out to get me? Maybe my dad didn't hit a moose—maybe he hit a car, or a kid? Maybe killed somebody? Maybe there's a family all enraged, with axes and rifles, sitting downstairs in the lobby—or whatever you call the place you sit in a hospital—waiting to come up and get their revenge? Like those crazy old villagers out to chop up the ogre. And one fat cop isn't going to be much help against a bunch of wild men out to chop up the kid whose dad killed their kid.

It's all I can think about—that cop and why he's out there. And my dad. I think about him too. It doesn't seem real that he's not here. Truth is, nothing does. Half the time it seems like I'm somebody else, floating up by the ceiling, looking down at some other poor kid lying in a bed in a hospital, who's thinking about his dad being dead. It's not me—I'm not even really here.

It's worst when I wake up at night and don't know where I am. Am I home? Then I see a railing on the bed. Is that real? I reach out to touch it. It's steel and cold. The cold feels good on my fingers 'cause it's so hot under the covers. Then it feels bad because I know this is real. My dad really is dead and won't come back. And then the cold sorta gets into my chest and gives me an ache so bad it makes me cry, but not loud enough for that cop to hear.

My biggest problem, besides thinking about the cop and my dad and the gang of people out to get me, is what to do with the key. It's not like any key I ever saw before. It's long and thin and brass, and it's got a number stamped at the top: *158*. Maybe it's for a locker? I don't know. What I do know is that I've gotta find a place to hide it, because it keeps slipping outta my hand when I fall asleep. But I don't have any pockets in this crazy gown, and my clothes aren't anywhere around the room, so where can I put it? Then I remember some old movie I saw.

"Nurse," I say, "could I have a Bible? Just to have beside me?"

"Sure. There's one in the table right beside you, my luv," she says, pulling it out of a drawer. "Do you want it open to any particular passage?"

I panic a bit, not knowing any particular passages. So I just say, "No—any old place," which isn't very religious-sounding. The nurse doesn't mind though, and she gives me a smile when she leaves, like she's thinking what a sweet kid I am. Soon as her back's turned, I get the key out and start prying up the thick paper inside the cover. Bit by bit I work the whole key inside, till just a bit of brass shows, which nobody would notice but me. For the rest of my time in the hospital I keep it right beside me—even the next day when the lady from Social Services shows up, with the fat cop right behind her.

He gives a snort when he sees me with the Bible.

"Sykes with a Bible—that's a first, wha?" he says with a mean kind of a laugh.

"Constable," the lady says, "if you have to be here, then you'll have to be quiet."

She sits down and gets out a big binder. She digs out a pen from a black bag on the floor, then lets out a big sigh and says, "Now, Charlie. My name is Kathleen Puddister, and I work with the provincial Child Services Department. We'll help look after you, now that your dad's...gone. To do that we need to know a little more about you."

"Like what?"

"Like where you live, for a start."

"Apartment 6B, 2719 West Third Street, Fort McMurray, Alberta, T9H 1B0."

"Very good" she says. "Not many boys as young as you would know their postal codes."

"I'm not young," I say. "I'm thirteen."

"Sorry. You look younger."

"Because I'm small," I say, which I know is true—smallest one in my class, every picture, until last year when that new kid moved in from India or somewheres they don't have enough food to get big. Or that's what my friend Robert says.

"So," she says, "you were born in Alberta?"

"Guess so. I'm not sure. I don't remember."

"No one remembers being born, Charlie."

"I mean later, like—I can't remember my mom or anything."

"And your dad didn't talk to you about your mother? What she was like?"

I shake my head.

"Nothing?"

"He didn't like to talk about her, because of what happened."

"And what did happen?"

"I don't know. He didn't like to talk about it, only to tell me she died."

"When you were a baby?"

"When I was a tiny baby, just born."

"All right," she says, smiling like she doesn't want to upset me with questions about my mom dying.

"And what about your dad—where was he born?"

"Out east, I guess. Out here."

"In Newfoundland?" she asks, which makes me want to ask a question myself.

"Mrs. Puddister," I say.

"Ms.," she says.

"Miz," I say. "Do *you* know where my father was born?"

The cop gives another laugh and gets a mean look from Miz.

"We're just verifying some things about your dad now, Charlie. We want to be sure just who you and your dad are."

"And who could we be?" I ask.

"Well," she says, slow, and seeming a bit confused herself. "It's just that it's important that we know exactly who people are when there's an accident like this. So we know who to contact, and what to tell them."

I don't say anything, so she goes on.

"You see, there were no documents in your car—no insurance papers, no registration. Which brings me to a few more questions about this trip you and your father were on. What can you tell me about it?"

Right away the cop gets his notebook out, and a funny thing happens. Everything slows down, like it does when you're in a fight at school. You see the other kid's stronger and that he's gonna smack you hard in the face, and all you can do is wait for the punch. Except I'm not waiting for a punch now. I'm waiting to decide what to say next. Whether I'll tell the truth.

The cop's just getting his pen out when I decide.

"Nothing to tell," I say.

"Was it a holiday, a vacation?" asks Miz.

I nod.

"Did your dad say why he was going to Newfoundland? To meet someone? A friend, maybe, or a relative?"

"Nope."

"Have you ever been here before?"

"Nope."

"So this was just a…a family vacation. No big deal?"

This second lie is easier—like the second time you jump off the high board.

"No big deal," I say, which is not the truth. The truth is my dad got a phone call just before we started on the trip. Late at night, when I was supposed to be in bed. Which I was, but I wasn't sleeping. At least not after the phone rang about twenty times. That's how I came to be listening when my dad talked to whoever was on the other end—just saying a few words, like "Okay" and "When?" and "Where?"

I could have told them about that, I guess. And about how I opened my door a crack to see if my dad was okay, 'cause he shut off the TV soon as he hung up. I could have told them about how he saw me looking at him and how his hands were shaking. And how he was all white, white like when you gotta stay home from school with the flu. And how he said to me, soon as he saw me, "Jesus, Charlie. We gotta go. We gotta start tomorrow. He's gettin' out…"

THREE

I first think about running away a couple a nights after they move me to the ward. The worst part of the ward isn't the noise—there's a lot of it, including a kid right next to me who pukes his guts up every couple of hours. Or the light out in the hallway, which shines just bright enough to creep in behind my eyelids when I almost fall asleep. The worst part is that my bed doesn't have a railing. Which is funny, because I never slept in a bed with a railing before. But that railing being there in the other bed, after my dad died, sorta made me feel safer somehow, once I got used to it—specially when I reached out to touch it. At night the moon came in just right to make it shine, and I could see finger-prints on it from where the doctors and nurses touched it. I'd rub 'em all off with my blanket and then see if I could make one perfect fingerprint, all the lines clear and sharp, like on those special maps—the topographic ones my dad used at work. But in the ward those railings were gone, and twice I almost fell outta bed. Or I dreamed I fell outta bed, which feels like the same thing when it wakes you up at some stupid time like 3:30 AM.

I know it's 3:30 because I can see the clock in the hallway, a big old one with black hands—same as the one outside the principal's office at school. That's what time it is when I hear them talking about me.

"He can't stay here," says one voice. He's just down the hall, outta sight. Gee, I think, lifting my head off the pillow so I can use both ears, don't those guys know I can hear them plain as anything? That I can hear the janitor squeeze out his mop two floors away at 3:33 AM?

"We'll need the bed on the weekend for sure," the voice goes on.

"They're looking," comes another voice, a nurse. "But it's not easy."

"Who's up on the foster list?"

"It's full."

"Well, The Hollow then."

"He's a kid, not a criminal."

A laugh from the man. "Well," he says, "we don't *know* that, do we? He's a Sykes. Anyway, they take overflow out there, don't they? In an emergency?"

"Used to."

"Well, leave a note for the day staff. I need the bed."

And that's the first time I think about running away. Not real serious, like thinking how I would do it, exactly, but more like realizing it was possible, you know? I mean, I don't even have a pair of pants. What would I do? Run down the road in a gown with my bum showing? No way. But I could.

Anyways, before I can plan anything out, Miz shows up next day to tell me I'm being moved. The fat cop's with her when she comes onto the ward, puffing away like he's just run up a mountain. Tubby would be a good name for him, I think. Constable Tubby.

"Charlie," says Miz, "we're moving you."

"Okay," I say.

"Don't you want to know where?" she asks, her eyebrows up.

"No," I say. "I don't know a good place from a bad place in Newfoundland."

"Well, the place we're sending you is a good place. And it's just for a bit, until we find you a place to live full-time. Usually we'd place you with a foster family for a few weeks while we found you a more permanent home. But our list of fosters is full, so we've got a spot for you at a provincial facility, the White Hills Training School."

"The Hollow?" I ask.

Miz drops her pen on the floor. I can see her look at Tubby when she bends over to pick it up. He's already got his notebook out.

"How do you know that name, Charlie?"

"That's what they call the place you're taking me, isn't it?"

She gives a nod. "That's what some of the children call it. But how do you know that name?"

"I just heard some of the...some of the kids talking about it."

"Children? In this ward?" Miz sounds like she doesn't quite believe me.

"Yeah," I say. "They—we—talk about all kinds of things. Hockey, movies, the place they put bad kids."

"But this is not a place for bad kids," says Miz, taking a minute to shoot a look at Tubby, who turns a laugh into a cough when he sees the glare on her face.

"It's a special school, with teachers trained to help children having...difficulties...getting along."

I don't nod or anything, just keep my face blank, like I do when I figure someone is lying to me. It's a good way to handle someone you think is maybe lying to you. That way they don't know if you believe them or not. And that makes them keep talking. And when they keep talking, they say the sorta thing that lets you know for sure if they're lying.

I wait.

"It really is quite a lovely spot," she says. "Really. I think you'll like it there."

See? Now I know. So I can ask a question.

"Miz," I say, "why do they call it The Hollow?"

"Well," she says, putting her papers back in the binder, being real busy so she doesn't have to look at me, "I think it's because of its setting. It's tucked away in the White Hills, in a little valley—sort of a hollow."

The cop lets out that cough again.

"The van will be here tomorrow at noon to pick you up," she says, heading for the door, Tubby behind her.

"It's a dark blue van with white writing on the side," he says before he follows her out. Then, quieter, to me, "It's got metal screens on the windows. Just so you know what to look for."

FOUR

The van pulls up right on time the next morning. I know because I'm wearing my dad's watch, which they gave to me when I signed out of the hospital. They gave me my clothes back, too, and my backpack. I can get the rest of my dad's stuff after the funeral, they said. But they say they don't know when that'll be, since they're still trying to talk to people in Fort McMurray. I also got the Bible, without even having to ask for it.

"It'll be a comfort," the nurse said when she handed it to me, which is true, since it means I don't have to find another place to hide the key.

The van is blue, just like Tubby said it would be. And it really does have metal screens on the windows, but there's no writing on it. Which seems funny to me. I mean, why not put writing on it? I guess they're trying to make it not stand out so much—make it look more like a bunch of kids out on a field trip. Except having metal screens around all the windows kind of spoils that, so why not write up what everyone can see? Put it in big letters: *Bus for Boys So Bad They Gotta Be Kept in a Cage.*

Miz stands with me at the curb when the van pulls into the parking lot and heads straight for us. Guess I might as well have writing on me too: *Orphan Kid Nobody Wants.* A second before the driver pulls up, Miz puts her hand on my shoulder, like I'm going to jump in front of it or something. You might think I'd yank myself away from her, but it feels kinda nice, and outta nowhere I almost start to cry, my eyes getting full. The weather isn't helping any since there's a wind blowing in my face; I haven't been outside in about a week, so I'm tearing up pretty good. I clamp my eyes shut real tight and turn my face while I mop up any water on my cheeks. I don't know much about Buses for Boys So Bad They Gotta Be Kept in a Cage, but I know you shouldn't get on one snot-nosed.

Tubby comes over to talk to the driver, who's outta the van, lighting up a cigarette.

"Mr. Rogers," a voice shouts from the van—a shout at the driver. "Billy Rogers! Give us one a them smokes."

More shouts: "Give us a drag, Billy." "Let's all of us have a pull, now!" "If ya don't got enough to share with everyone, don't be bringing 'em out at all."

The shouts shift to Miz when the boys spot her.

"Who's yer girlfriend, Billy?" comes a call. Then another one, "Miss, miss, show us yer—"

"Enough," the driver snaps. "Little shits," he says, real quiet. He gives the van a glare, then seeing Miz pawing around the bottom of her bag for a pen, he tosses a quick finger back at the boys. And it's like something explodes far off, behind a closed door. Yells, shouts, laughing, the van rocking side to side.

"Jesus," Tubby says to the driver. "Better you than me."

"Three more years, b'y. Then I'm done and off to the country."

The driver looks at me for the first time. "Better get you aboard," he says, unlocking the back door. "Find a seat and sit down. I'll do roll call in a minute."

The hollering stops soon as I get aboard, with everyone turning to look at me. It stinks inside—sweat from big boys and something else I don't want to think about. There's one seat left, on the aisle at the very front, where a fat kid's scrunched up against the window. All the eyes go from me up to the empty seat when I head for it. Then I see what stinks: puke, all over that one seat. I swallow hard just looking at it; no way I'm sitting there.

"Better sit down," a kid calls out from the back. "Billy can't move this thing till everyone's sat down."

"That's right," says a kid across the aisle in the other front window seat—the one who called for the cigarette. "Little runt like you don't want to get Billy pissed at him."

"Too late," says a third kid. "Here he comes, and he's got that look."

A minute later the driver's in his seat, turning round to slide open a plastic panel between the front and back of the van.

"Jesus," he says. "What died back there?"

There's a burst of noise as the boys all call out an answer.

"All right, shut up!" he shouts. "If ye crowd aren't quiet in five seconds, I'll take the shore road back, and it won't just be Pillsbury here pukin' his guts up.

"Now," he says once they settle down, "I'll do the roll. Butt, Corey?"

"Yup," says a skinny kid who's holding up a booger he just slid outta his nose.

"Crocker, Danny?"

"What're ya at?" comes a call back.

It goes on, down to Walsh, Frankie.

No answer. I see the driver turn his head to look at the kid in the front seat, the one across the aisle. Walsh, Frankie turns toward the driver and they stare at each other. The kid is chewing something, his mouth scrinched up in a rat nibble, like when you got a hangnail between your teeth. He tilts his head, pokes the tip of his tongue out and gives a spit—a little pop.

"Present," he says.

The driver checks off his name.

"And you, new kid," he says to me. "Sykes, Charlie."

"Here," I say. I expect more hoots, but instead there's just a bunch of whispers.

"Sykes," says Walsh, Frankie once Billy slides the little window shut. "You really a Sykes?"

I nod.

"I ain't never heard of a Charlie Sykes."

"I'm not from here. I'm from Alberta."

"You're the kid in that accident—the orphan kid whose old man got killed by the moose. I seen it on the news."

He nods to himself.

"Gameboy," he says, turning round to a kid behind him wearing a big pair of glasses on even bigger ears. "Switch seats with him."

"No way," says Gameboy. "I ain't sitting in Pillsbury puke."

Walsh, Frankie turns all the way round in his seat and grabs Gameboy's ear, pinching the bottom tight. I look to see what the driver's going to do, but he's turned the other way, signing some papers. Walsh, Frankie's got Gameboy pulled close to him now, close enough to whisper something in his ear. Then he pushes him away and swats him in the head, knocking his glasses onto the floor.

"Next time I'll tear it right off," he says, turning round to face forward. Gameboy bends over to feel for his glasses, patting the floor till he finds them, then gets up and shoves past me toward the puke seat, where he sits, as close to the edge as he can.

"You're a real prick, you know that, Walsh?" Gameboy says across the aisle. He just whispers it, in a hiss. Walsh, Frankie doesn't say anything back. He just nods as I sit in the seat behind him. I figure he knows what he is.

FIVE

I get my first look at The Hollow just after one o'clock that afternoon. It doesn't seem too bad. Flat roof, red and brown bricks, lots of windows—all of them long, tall and narrow, sorta like a castle with the top chopped off. And lots of lawn running up to it, cut nice, with some flowers and stuff. It looks sorta like a golf course, except for the big chain-link fence around everything. It's like those screens on the bus: normal, wrapped in steel.

I don't like it.

At least I won't have to be here long, I think, as I watch the other kids pile outta the van. Gameboy first, puking on the grass soon as he hits fresh air. Pillsbury's the last one out, and he flops on the lawn while the other kids line up at the door.

"Serves ya right for eatin' all a them pancakes," says Nose Picker. "Disgusting what you shoves in yer face."

"That's enough," says the driver, pressing a button by the door that sets off a buzzer. "You got an hour of class left, so drop your court documents at the office and get to class. Except you, Sykes. You come with me."

We go down a long hallway that ends at an office with glass walls—I can see right inside to where a guy's sitting at a big desk. He waves us in.

"Have a seat," he says to me. Then to the driver, "That's all, Billy. Thanks."

He swivels his chair toward me.

"I've just been reading your file," he says, taking off his glasses. "Sorry about your dad. That can't be easy. And it can't be easy ending up here, not that here's such a bad place."

"Got a nice lawn," I say.

"Nicer than mine. The boys mow it, weed it. Not that you'll be doing that. We expect you'll just be here for a week, maybe two, while we straighten out your family situation."

"About that, Mister…"

"Delaney. My name is Gordon Delaney. I'm superintendent here—like a principal, with a few more keys."

He smiles, like we're buddies. But he doesn't put out his hand for me to shake.

"You were asking…," he says.

"About my family thing."

"The situation," says Delaney. "It's…ah…"

He lets out a big breath of air.

"It's complicated. What do you know about your family, Charlie?"

"Nothing. I got my dad; I had my dad."

"No cousins, uncles, anybody your dad spoke of?"

"No."

Mr. Delaney gives his chin a good long rub. I can hear the *scritch-scratch*. It makes me think of my dad, and I feel my eyes getting watery again. But there's no wind to blame it on now, so I have to figure out some other way to keep solid inside. I listen real close to every word Delaney's saying, concentrating on that.

"We, or I should say the Department of Child Services, believes you may have some family members here, Charlie. The issue, ah…"

He's all stumbly when he's talking, looking at me, looking at the ceiling.

"The thing is, we have to determine…suitability." He sighs again. "Do you understand?"

I shake my head.

"Your father," he starts. Then he grunts. Really. Let's out this old-man grunt, then doesn't say anything for a minute or two. Long enough that he lines up six pencils in a straight row on his desk. Then he says, "I can tell you this much: Your dad was born in Newfoundland, in St. John's. He has some family here, and we're in the process of tracking them down, talking with them, seeing if they'd be willing and able to take in a young boy."

"Me."

"You."

"And if they can't?" I say.

"Then we'd look for another home."

"A foster home?"

"Charlie," says Delaney, "all this is the responsibility of Child Services. They can answer your questions. In fact, they've set up a meeting with you for tomorrow morning, here at the school. Maybe they'll have some answers then. I can't say much more than what I've told you."

He slips his shirt sleeve back to look at his watch, then presses a button on his desk. It doesn't make any noise I can hear, but you can bet there's a buzzer going off somewheres.

"For now, we'll get you settled in your room. I've got an older student who'll show you where you'll sleep. Here he is now—Simon."

Pillsbury comes through the door, wearing a new shirt, face washed, hair wet.

"Simon, this is Charlie Sykes. He'll be here a few days, up in Brookside. Room three. Thanks."

It doesn't take long for Pillsbury to work up a sweat. By the time we walk down a couple of hallways and up a flight of stairs, he can hardly talk. When we pass through a big set of doors into an open area that's got *Brookside* written at one end, he's puffing worse than Tubby.

"Here ya go," he manages, opening the door to Room 3. "You sleep in here."

Room 3 is long and narrow, shaped just like the window that sits at the far end of it. On one side there's a little bed, and across from that there's a chair, a desk and a lamp.

Everything else is bare: the walls, the floor, the closet and hangers—like nobody's ever been in it before, except I can tell they have because there are chips on the paint and scuffs on the floor. But there's nothing else to let you know another kid ever slept here or read a book here or laughed at a joke.

Hollow.

"Unpack your stuff," says Pillsbury. "Class'll be out in a bit; then there'll be a buzzer for supper. Everybody'll head down to the cafeteria—just look for me if your wondering which way to go."

Yeah, I think, you'll be at the head of the line—though I don't say anything but "'Kay."

Pillsbury heads off, and I start to unpack. A pair of jeans, a couple of T-shirts—just what I had when we left Fort Mac.

It's weird looking at the stuff, because it makes me think how my dad was alive the last time I saw it. And that makes me sad, thinking about putting it away in a closet or a dresser, which I know is kind of stupid. I mean, it's not like my dad folded it up for me or anything soppy like that. I mean, my jeans are rolled up in a ball in the pack, and I did the laundry myself before we left. Still, the last time the clothes were in fresh air my dad was breathing it. It's a funny feeling.

I decide to keep one T-shirt folded up, just like it was when I packed it. It's an Edmonton Oilers T-shirt my dad wore to work until it got a hole in the armpit. After that I wore it to bed whenever he worked a night shift. I put the rest of the stuff in the closet, which I kinda hate doing.

Putting stuff away is like staying at…I don't know, a grandma's house at the ocean, I'd guess, when you go for the summer. I've never done that, but I've imagined doing it sometimes, usually just before school lets out for the summer. And now maybe I could have a grandma out here. I can't imagine that, though, because I never seen a picture of anyone in the family except my dad. Not even my mom.

"Didn't have a camera," my dad said the one time I asked about it. "Didn't want one," he added on, when it looked like I had a few more questions bubbling up.

Without a picture, I don't even know what my mom looked like, though I've got a way to try and guess how she might have looked. It works like this: I get a quiet time, like after school when my dad won't be home for a while. Then I get up close to a mirror and look at my face. And in my mind I take away the parts that look like my dad. Then I try to put together the pieces left over and see what my mom musta looked like. Try it sometime. It's hard. Sometimes I can't even see the parts of me that look like my dad, except we both have dimples and lips that look kinda the same. And a forehead that goes a long way up before it hits hair.

There's a mirror in this room, so I look in it. For a sec I can't see anything that looks like my dad, but then I see the dimple. Some day I'll start shaving and my chin will have that *scritch-scratch* sound like my dad's when I rub it.

"Oh, you're real pretty," comes a voice from the doorway. A big kid strolls in. Other kids are coming into the common area behind him. Class must be out. He gives me a bump as he walks in front of the mirror and bends his face close to it.

"Not as pretty as me though."

He tilts his chin up and squeezes a zit—*bam*—all over the mirror.

"That's better," he says, flopping onto the bed—my bed, I think about saying. But he's big, with hair on his knuckles and his chin. Sixteen at least, I figure.

"What's yer name, new kid?"

"Charlie."

"Little Charlie Tucker," he sings out, like it's a nursery rhyme, "was a nasty little…"

He spots the Bible on the desk.

"What's this?" he says, sitting up to grab it.

"Nothing."

"Nothing, my arse," he says, flipping it open.

"Hey, Brother Ribs," he yells to a kid in the hallway. "Come in here. We're going to have us a little reading."

A skinny kid comes in, T-shirt down to his knees. He's smaller than me, the shirt hanging off him like something a crazy old man would wear, all pulled outta shape and droopy.

"What's a reading?" says Ribs.

"From the Bible," says the big kid. "I'll be the priest, and you—new kid—you be the sinner. Get down on yer knees."

I let out a big sigh and look at the door. A couple more kids are standing there, poking one another, looking like they're gonna laugh.

"I don't want trouble," I say. All I can think about is that brass key bouncing on the tiles after it falls outta the cover. "I just want you to put the book down. Okay?"

"There's no trouble," says the big kid. He's all smiley now and steps closer. "You just needs to get down on yer knees to say a prayer, Charlie. That's all."

He puts a hand on my shoulder. He's strong—I can tell right away when he presses me down without even trying. Then all of a sudden he kicks at my leg, right behind my knee, and I fall.

"Jesus," I say.

"Ah, ah, Charlie—mustn't take the Lord's name in vain. You'll get a beating if ya keeps that up."

He looks over at Ribs, his hand still pressed on my shoulder.

"We got a priest. We got a sinner. We need a nun," he says. "You, Ribs, that shirt yer wearing is half a dress anyways. Ya just need a thing to put round yer head."

He reaches onto the bed and grabs my dad's Oilers T-shirt.

"Wrap that round yer head—like one a them Eye-Rack towel-heads…"

It's too much, seeing that shirt getting tossed. I scrinch out from under the big kid's hand and grab the shirt from Ribs.

"Piss off," I shout. "Leave my stuff alone."

"Piss off?" the big kid laughs. "Your stuff?"

He looks around the room.

"What the hell do you think belongs to you in this room, little Charlie?"

He takes a swipe at the lamp on the desk and knocks it over. "The light?"

He grabs the bed covers and yanks them off with one pull, chucking them on the floor. "The sheets?"

He walks right on top of them and goes to the closet where he yanks my stuff off the hangers and drops it on the floor, slamming the door shut so hard that it shakes a big cloud of dust loose from the ceiling tiles. The dust floats down through a patch of sun coming through the window, all sparkly.

"What do you think belongs to you?" he shouts again. "Nuddin', b'y—it all belongs to the Department of Youth Corrections. And what don't belong to them belongs to me."

He's got me by the front of my shirt now, both his paws pulling on it, stretching it out in front of my face.

"Do you got it?"

"It doesn't," I manage to say. My legs are trembling so bad I can barely stand.

"What?" yells Big Kid. "Say that again, b'y—go on."

"It doesn't belong to you," I say, yelling myself now. "That's my stuff—that's my shirt and that's my Bible!"

Big Kid throws me back, banging me against the closet door.

"You little shit," he says. There's spit bubbling on his lips. He pulls his hand back, light from the window catching the hairs on it, black as wires. Then another fist, a different one, flies straight into Big Kid's face, and right behind it comes Walsh, Frankie, falling on top of Big Kid as hard as he can.

Walsh, Frankie pulls his elbow all the way back and hits
Big Kid once, twice, three, four, five times—*bam, bam, bam,
bam, bam*—as fast and hard as he can. The bubbles from
Big Kid's mouth are bright red now, and I feel sick—so sick
I gotta sit down.

"More?" shouts Walsh, Frankie. "Ya big, stupid git. Want
some more?"

Before Big Kid can say anything, two guys fly into the
room—grown-ups, their shirt backs spread tight across their
shoulders as they both grab on to Walsh, Frankie and throw
him across the room.

"Enough, Walsh!" one shouts while the other bends over
Big Kid. His white shirt has red streaks all down the front
when he stands up.

"Call the infirmary," he says to his partner as he helps
Big Kid to his knees. "It'll be stitches, for sure. And you," he
says to Walsh, Frankie, "you stay right where you're to till
I get back."

Then, just like that, everything goes quiet. I'm still on the
floor, and Walsh, Frankie is sitting on the bed, wiping blood
from his knuckles onto his jeans. He sees me looking at him.

"Wha?"

I don't say anything, so he asks again, "Wha?"

"Thanks. I guess."

He laughs. "My pleasure. I been waiting six months for
a reason to give that Baywop a smack."

"Baywop?"

"You really are from Alberta, aren't ya, Cowboy?" he says. "Baywop—somebody from around the Bay, outside St. John's. A hick."

He stops for a minute to shake his hand.

"Ah, Jesus, that stings," he says. "This particular stunned arsehole comes from back a beyond down the South Coast. The outskirts of Burgeo. Flarehead, we calls him—'cause ya never know what's going to set him off. He's a bad piece of work—leastways, when he's in a racket with someone smaller than him—which is most of the time."

"You're smaller," I say.

"I'm shorter," says Walsh, Frankie. "But I'm bigger here," he says, pointing to his arm. "Older too—almost eighteen."

He gives his hand a last wipe and puts it out for me to shake.

"I'm Frankie, Frankie Walsh."

I shake it. It's strong and hard, like it should be attached to somebody older.

"Some of the crowd here calls me Present," he says.

"Present?"

"Because I'm always here," says Frankie. "And I'll be here a while longer, after this little racket."

He rubs his hand.

"It's worth an extra few days inside to give that Flarehead a bit a what he's always handing out. The prick."

A man comes to the door—the one who took Flarehead to the infirmary.

"All right, Walsh," he says. "Let's go."

Frankie gets to his feet and heads for the door but stops before he steps out.

"Cowboy," he says, turning back to me. "Ya owes me one now."

I nod, and then he's gone.

SIX

Supper's all right—fish sticks and French fries. That's better than the hospital, which always ended with Jell-O, which is just ground-up cows. It's true. Robert says they make it at the same exact factory where they make Elmer's glue, except the conveyor belt goes off in two directions: one way the stuff gets turned into glue for schools, the other way the stuff gets dumped full of sugar and food coloring and goes to grocery stores. And to hospitals.

Anyways, supper's over at six and after that it's free time— that's what the counselor called it, which seems stupid to me since all you're free to do is watch some crappy TV channel or bat around a Ping-Pong ball with a big dent in it that makes it bounce all crazy.

"Used to be a pool table," Pillsbury tells me, "till they busted up all the cues."

Finally I get so bored I go back to my room and start reading the Bible, after I check to make sure the key's okay for about the twentieth time that day. I look for that Revelation stuff, about how the world gets blown up, but once I start reading, it's mostly about Alphas and Omegas, which is pretty boring. I turn back to the start, about God creating the world and making light outta the void. I don't even really know what a void is, except it's something empty and dark and scary—kinda like where I was right after the accident.

I guess I fall asleep reading, because when I open my eyes all the lights are out and the Bible's sitting open on my chest. I put it under my pillow, then lay back, looking at the window. It's like all the other windows, long and skinny—too skinny for even a kid like Ribs to crawl through. And it's sparkly too, I see in the moonlight, getting up to have a better look. Up close I see it's got tiny silver wires running through it—little, tiny bars. While I'm looking I hear a noise so soft it's not like a real noise at first, more like a change in the quiet. Even so, I know it right away: it's somebody crying, trying hard to make sure nobody else hears.

I step into the hallway to listen at the room next door. Just snores. Same in the next. Then three doors down I hear the crying stop just when I stand in the doorway. I listen hard; there's a snort—somebody snuffling back the snot.

"You okay?" I whisper.

Nothing.

"You all right?" I whisper again.

There's another snuffle, then I see a bit of dark sit up in the bed. "Who's that?" it asks.

"Me. The new kid. Charlie."

"Whaddaya want?"

"Nothing. Just thought maybe somebody was crying."

"I ain't crying," says the voice.

My eyes are getting used to the dim, and I can see the kid better. It's gotta be Ribs—I see a skinny arm shoot under the covers, hiding something.

"You should mind your own business," he says. "Mind your business and go back to bed."

"'Kay. Just thought maybe I could help."

"You can help by getting outta here."

"'Kay," I say again and head back to my room.

It takes me a long time to get to sleep, looking at the moon shining off those tiny bars in that skinny window.

SEVEN

Flarehead isn't at breakfast next morning, which is good. But neither is Frankie Walsh, which I figure is not so good. For him at least. Ribs is, though, and he's sitting alone. I sit down across from him.

"Hey," I say. "Where'd ya get the Fruit Loops?"

"They ain't Fruit Loops," says Ribs. "They're No Name Rainbow Circles, and they suck."

I nod.

"Tough to sleep in here, isn't it? Lots of noise," I say.

"I don't hear nothing at night," says Ribs, giving me a stare. "And you don't neither."

He stands up to move to another table.

"And don't be talking to me," he says in a whisper. "You're a dead man when Flarehead gets outta the stitch shop."

"I never touched him. He's the one—"

"Yeah, yeah," Ribs says. "Tell it to him when he's twisting yer neck off, New Kid. I mean it—you're dead."

I don't get a chance to say anything to that, because all of a sudden Mr. Delaney walks up.

"Charlie," he says. "You and I have got a meeting with Child Services in about two minutes. Finish up and c'mon. It won't take long, and you can join up with a class after."

"'Kay. Where should I put the tray?"

"Just leave it," says Delaney. "I'll get Simon to take it up."

Pillsbury's shoving my toast into his face before me and Delaney even leave the cafeteria.

"The board room's right here," says Delaney, opening a door after we go round a corner or two. I step inside, and there's Miz, her big bag on the table and a couple of binders open beside it. I look for Tubby, but he's not here. Some other guy is, though, 'bout as old as my dad, wearing jeans and a stripy shirt. His hair is all messy like they wear it on TV, so you can't tell if it's messy on purpose or messy because they just got outta bed. But this guy smells like soap and shampoo, not old bedsheets, so I figure it's messy on purpose.

"You must be Charlie," he says, holding out his hand for me to shake. It's soft and sweaty but cold, like a dishcloth sitting by the sink.

"My name is Desmond—Desmond Fitzpatrick. You can call me Dez. I've been assigned—actually I've asked to be assigned—to your case. My job is to be your advocate at Child Services."

I have to give my hand a bit of a pull to get it loose.

"Do you know what an advocate is, Charlie?" he asks.

I give him my blank look.

"It means I look out for your interests."

I keep it blank.

"I'm on your side," he says, giving me a little point with his finger when he says *your*. "Looking out for what's best for Charlie Sykes."

"Okay," I say, sitting down in a chair beside him.

"Charlie," he says, pulling a folder out of a briefcase, "you know we've been looking for family members of yours in Alberta. Well, we haven't found any."

"How'd you do something like that?" I ask.

"Sorry," says Dez. "Something like…?"

"Look for 'em. You'd use computers and stuff?"

Dez nods. "Government records, on computer."

"So," I say, then stop. I don't know if I really want to ask what I sorta want to ask.

"It's okay, Charlie," says Dez. "You can ask about anything."

I still don't know if I want to ask about this thing—this little hope I have…not a hope, exactly. I don't know what to call it. A little thing I think about when I feel lonely. Do you know what I mean, lonely? Like at 5:30 on a Friday, at suppertime, when I'm waiting for my dad, and he isn't coming home. And there's no one around to call because they're all home eating their suppers or out bowling with their moms and dads or getting into their minivans to go out to see a movie. That's when I feel that kind of lonely—a deep lonely right inside my chest, so that it's a kind of a hurt. I don't have a word for it exactly, but *void* comes pretty close. And the only thing that makes me feel a bit better is this little hope I have. It's a thought I have about my mom—that she might be out there, somehow, somewhere, and that she might be looking for me. Which is stupid, I know, because my dad told me she's dead. But as long as I don't know for sure, then *maybe* it could be true. And I need a little something like that bit of hope right now, if you know what I mean.

"Nothing," I say.

"You sure?" asks Dez. "Because we can discuss anything you're concerned about…Nothing? Okay. So, nobody in Alberta. But you do have some family here in Newfoundland, which I guess you didn't know about."

I shake my head. "My dad never told me about anybody else, except my mom, and how she died when I was just born."

"Well," Dez says, "your dad did have a family. He had a mom and a dad, Dick and Doreen, who are both dead now. There is a cousin, who we're having discussions with, but she's elderly—in her seventies—and it's unlikely she'd be able to care for a twelve-year-old on her own."

"I'm not twelve," I say. "I'm thirteen. I been thirteen for over half a year, so I'm really closer to fourteen than thirteen."

"Sorry," says Dez. "Thirteen. Anyway, there's also a brother."

"A brother? I got a brother?"

"Sorry," he says. "I mean your dad had a brother. Nick. You never heard of him?"

"No. Is he around? Could I...?"

Dez starts to say something but has to stop to clear his throat with a noise that sounds like a cat puking up a hair ball. He tries again.

"Nick is, ah...not able, at this time, to take you in."

"How come?"

There's a long pause, with Miz finally throwing out an answer. "He doesn't have a home right now."

"How come?"

"He's in a supported-living environment at the moment," says Dez.

"A what?"

"A supported-living environment," he says again.

"Like, on a machine?"

"No, no," Dez says. "In a place with some other people, so he doesn't have a room he could put you in. That kind of thing."

"So will he be getting one—a room? For himself?"

"Not," says Dez, who's not talking as smooth as when we first sat down, "in the foreseeable future."

"So not for a while," I say.

"No."

"So what happens to me?"

"Well, your cousin may be able to help there—to take you in."

"But what if she can't?"

"Then you'd stay here—just for a bit, till we arrange a foster situation for you."

"Like a fake family?"

"Not fake," says Miz. "Temporary."

"Like, just for a bit," I say.

"Charlie," says Dez, leaning toward me and getting his smooth sound back again. "I know this is difficult, but we're doing the best we can—making sure you're safe and cared for."

I think about telling him about the fight last night, but figure no, I'll just say nothing. Let him go on.

"You really are our top priority. That's the bottom line for us, and we'll let you know about any change that's coming just as soon as we know it ourselves."

He looks over at Miz when he finishes, like he's expecting a grade for something.

"Do you have any questions?" he says.

"No," I say, which isn't true. I got about a million, starting with who Nick Sykes is, and why he hasn't got his own room when he's forty-five years old? Maybe he's retarded, living with a bunch of other retarded guys who drive around on a bus—probably without any writing on it either. If he's not retarded, then how come he can't go live with that old aunt and look after me from her house? But I figure I won't get a real answer to any of that, so I don't say anything.

"Well," says Dez, "that's it for today. Child Services will be in touch as soon as there's any news. In the meantime, you can take my card and call me anytime you need anything. My number's at the bottom."

Which is fine, I think, putting the card in my pocket, except that's one thing I haven't seen in here—a phone. Not on the wall, not on a kid. Which makes the number about as good as a parachute on a space shuttle.

"You okay, Charlie?" Dez asks.

"Yeah," I say.

"You thinking about your dad?"

"No."

"Because if you are, you know, thinking about him, or feeling sad or angry or want to talk to anyone, we can arrange that."

"No."

"Well," says Mr. Delaney, "if we're done here, I'll show Charlie to his class."

A minute later, me and Mr. Delaney are at another door. Mr. Delaney gives it a knock.

"Mr. Aikens," he says, sticking his head in the class. "Sorry to interrupt. I've got a new student for you—Charlie Sykes, just here for a few days. I'd like him to sit in on classes."

"Sure," Mr. Aikens says to me. "Find a seat."

"Watch out for the puke," calls a kid I recognize from the bus. They all laugh, but quiet, down into their books. I sit down and see why: there's Frankie, turned around in his front-row seat, giving them a glare. His knuckles are two shades of red, deeper in the middle, no bandages or anything. And he's got a bruise on his face that I don't remember from yesterday.

"All right," says the teacher. "Back to you, Mr. Walsh. The first word again."

Frankie starts reading from a book, "Wh...wh..."

He's got one hand on the book, the other in his hair, twirling it around so it's a big heap on top of his head—like something Dez would pay a lot of money for.

"Jesus," Frankie says after another couple of tries. "It ain't no word I ever seen before."

The teacher takes the book from him and drops it on my desk. There's a red smear where Frankie's been holding it.

"You try, Mr. Sykes."

"Winter comes early to Newfoundland," I read. "Snow is often recorded in early October and usually covers the island by mid-December."

Frankie comes up to me when class is over, half an hour later.

"You read good," he says.

"I guess."

"No, b'y, you do. Quick, like. You make them sentences sound good. How they go up and down, like you were really talking. That's good."

"I like to read."

"I hates it," says Frankie. He gives me a nod to come over closer.

"So listen," he says. "I needs you to do a favor for me—after I done one for you last night, right?"

I nod.

"But I don't wants ta talk here—too many teachers. We'll meet up this afternoon. Outside."

"We can meet outside?"

"Sure," says Frankie. "Just tell 'em you wants to go landscaping in third period. Tell Aikens—he don't care what ya do. I'll be out there, keeping an eye for ya. By the Catwalk."

"The what?" I ask, but it's too late. He's already off down the hall.

I go outside after second period, but there's no Frankie around, so I ask Nose Picker if he's seen him.

"I'm looking for Frankie," I say. "He said to meet him at the Catwalk."

"I bet he did," says Nose Picker. He gives a nod back behind The Hollow. "Catwalk's out back. He'll be down on all fours, sniffing round."

The kids standing around Nose Picker start giggling, and one lets out a howl like a wolf might do. Weird bunch, but they're right about Frankie—he's around back, talking to Gameboy, each of them holding a rake.

"Cowboy," Frankie calls out when he sees me.

"Hey," I say. They're leaning against a wood railing that runs along a boardwalk. It's a nice boardwalk, the wood all cut square. And it's clean, like nobody ever walks on it. It goes up the hill behind The Hollow, toward a back fence, and ends at a gate with a bunch of streetlights above it.

"This the Catwalk?" I say.

"It is," says Frankie.

"Why's it called that?"

"Because of what's at the other end," says Gameboy.

Frankie gives a laugh. Then another one when he sees I don't know what he's talking about.

"Pussy," Frankie says, smiling the kind of smile I only ever see on grown-ups. I can guess what he means, even though I'm not sure exactly why.

"Girls," I say.

Frankie nods and Gameboy gives a howl, just like the kid out front.

"You mean there's a place like this—a Hollow—for girls?"

"Not like this," says Frankie. "This here is for kids doing a sentence, for B and Es, assault, selling dope. Over there, it's more for Emo girls—cutters, pukers, dopers. Sorta like a rehab—a low-end mental."

"You ever talk to them?" I ask, which gets Gameboy howling again.

"Not allowed to," says Frankie, aiming a swat at Gameboy.

"But Frankie do," says Gameboy, dancing away from the swing.

"Sometimes," Frankie says with that smile again. "But we get in shit if we're caught up there. We're a bad influence. Anyways, most of them ain't worth talking to. They're crazy, or retarded—worse than us down here."

"'Cept they smell better," says Gameboy. "An' they got tits."

"All right," says Frankie, not smiling. He reaches into his jacket and gets out a plastic pencil case. He pulls out a cigarette and tosses it underhand to Gameboy.

"Go smoke that somewheres else," he says and gives a nod for Gameboy to take off, which he does. He pulls two more smokes from the case and points one at me.

I shake my head. "I don't smoke."

"Never?"

"Nope."

"Wanna try?"

I do kinda. My dad used to smoke when he'd come home late. In winter I'd hear the truck pull in, then the snow scrunching on the back deck, him standing there—"Having a draw," he'd say—rocking back and forth in the freezin' cold, one foot to the other, *scrinch, scrunch*. In the summer there'd be no noise, but I could smell it, floating through the window. I liked that smell, just after the smoke first got lit. But then we saw this picture in health class of a smoker's lung—all black and bumpy. There's more than four thousand chemicals in each puff. Stuff you'd never think would be in a cigarette, which looks sorta clean and safe wrapped up in all that white paper. Stuff like arsenic and lead and tar—just like what comes outta oil sands. Except it goes into your lungs. No thanks, I said after that class. Deep down I think I say no because I'm scared to try, which would make it brave to try. Right? Or would it be stupid? Can you be brave and stupid, all at once? I think maybe you can. But mostly I'm just scared, so I say no again.

"'Kay," says Frankie. He puts the extra smoke away and bends his head into his hand, flicks the lighter and pulls in that first draw. He lets it out, and the wind takes it past my head. It smells good.

"Okay, Cowboy," he says. "Remember how I said you owes me one? So here's the deal. Because of that fight last night, they wants to give me extra time inside, which they can't do—only a judge can do that. Except they got a way to get around that."

He takes another pull, squinting when the wind blows the smoke back in his face.

"What they do is, they make you meet your probation rules, exactly. Which for me means I gotta pass a reading test—reading comprehension they calls it. It's always been in my probation order—that I gotta go to school inside, and that I gotta achieve grade five reading comprehension or something. I never paid no attention to it, and neither did they. Except now, when they wants to let me know who's boss, they dig this out and say I can't get outta here till I pass this test, which there's no way I can do."

"So," I say, kinda surprised a kid as big and old as Frankie Walsh can't read like a grade five, "you want me to help you study?"

Smoke comes pop-pop-popping outta Frankie's mouth when he starts to laugh.

"No, no, Cowboy, you don't get it. Listen to what I'm sayin'. There's no way I can pass that test."

"But what if we start with some easy stuff."

Frankie lets out a big sigh. Seems everybody lets out a big sigh when they figure they've gotta explain something to me. He flicks the smoke onto the Catwalk. It sits there, still going, in the sun. The smoke curls up a little ways, then gets caught by the wind. I think I should step on it, but figure I better pay attention to Frankie first.

"Listen, Cowboy," says Frankie, giving me a poke in the shoulder. "I gotta prove I can read to get outta this place. But I *can't* read. And I'm not gonna learn to read. Right? So you gotta do it for me."

"Whaddaya mean?"

"I mean you gotta write that test for me."

"Cheat, you mean?"

Frankie gives another laugh.

"Cheat?" he says. "What's cheatin', Cowboy? Does you even know what it means? Because I'll tell what cheatin' is to me. Cheatin's when my old man takes the money what's supposed to buy our dinner and spends it on Black Horse and Pro-line and gives me a smack when he loses all his bets. That's cheatin'. What I'm talkin' about doin' is the opposite— it's doin' the right thing. It's helpin' him what helped you. I get you outta a hard spot, you get me outta a hard spot. How's that cheatin'?"

"But it's me doing your work."

"That's right," says Frankie. "Just like I done your work last night. With this."

He holds up the bloody hand, then puts it round mine. "And you gotta use this"—he shakes both our hands—"to write that test."

He lets my hand go.

"Not perfect, mind—I just needs fifty plus one."

"But how am I going to write a test for you?"

"Don't worry about that—I'll get everything to you. You just needs to fill it out and give it back to me. Nobody'll ever know anything, 'cept me and thee."

He grabs the rake off the railing.

"I'll get it to you tomorrow, an' you can look it over. I'm goin' back out front now, but you stay here for a bit—don't want Billy or Delaney to know we been hangin' out. Okay?"

I nod.

"Okay," says Frankie. "See ya."

I don't bother looking after him. Instead, I look for the cigarette, which the wind's blown up the Catwalk. I hate litter. I don't know why—guess it's something I got from my dad. He always used to pick up any garbage he'd see laying around.

"Take care of your own crap," he'd say.

So I take a few steps on the Catwalk to pick up that smoke, which is cold now. I bend down to grab it and shove it in my pocket. When I stand up, off in the distance there's someone looking down at me from the locked gate at the top of the hill. It's a girl at the far end of the Catwalk, staring at me through the fence. She's a ways away, so I can't really tell what she looks like, but she looks nice, standing there, soft against the hard fence. She's got jeans on and a brown jacket, zipped up against the wind. We look at each other for a bit. Should I wave? I want to. But I wait. Maybe she'll wave first. I think she's going to—but no, she's just brushing her hair outta her face. Of course she doesn't wave—why would she wave at some stupid little kid who's out picking up some big kid's old cigarette? Still, she might, I think, and I get ready to wave back, just in case. But she doesn't move. I don't know how long we stand like that, waiting. All of a sudden I turn round and start inside. Better to turn away before she does.

EIGHT

It's suppertime when I go in, everybody heading for the cafeteria. I go to the bathroom first, though, to wash my hands after picking up that butt. I'm squishing the bubbles through my fingers when all of a sudden the lights go out, and a second later two arms grab me in a bear hug. It's Flarehead. "I owe you something, Puke Pants," he says, reaching down to grab my hands. Still holding me tight from behind, he starts squeezing, his fat paw squishing my fingers so hard I can feel my knuckles crushing together. My fingers are slippery from the soap, though, and a second later I pull 'em free, giving Flarehead a faceful of soapy water when I yank my arm back.

"You little prick," he says, wiping soap from his eyes. I back toward the door.

"Go on," he says. "Run to your buddy, Frankie. But I'll tell you something before you go, Puke Pants. Frankie's gettin' outta here in a couple a days, and when he goes, it'll be just you and me. And I'm gonna break yer neck, you hear me, Puke Pants? And I know just how to do it, 'cause I done it before."

"You're crazy," I say, closer to the door all the time.

"You're right—I'm crazy. Got a piece of paper to prove it too—signed by a doctor. And soon as Frankie boy walks out the front door, I'm coming for you."

All of a sudden his arm shoots out, but instead of grabbing me, he yanks the door open.

"Go on," he says. "Get out. Plenty of time to get you. I ain't going nowhere, and neither are you."

———

Nothing's broke, I don't think, when I look at my fingers later. A couple of them look bent a bit, but I can wiggle them. It feels better when I rub them, just a little bit, which I do while I try to fall asleep.

You know the saddest thing I think of, lying in this bed? Sadder than my hand hurting or having a crazy bully planning to break my neck or being stuck in a boys' reform school? It's that nobody cares about me in this place. Not one person who wants to see me. Not one person who'd smile if they saw me come round a corner.

The moon is coming through the window again tonight, making stuff white and gray in millions of little dots. It's bright enough I can see the time on my dad's watch—*1:15*. I bet I could almost read the Bible if I tried, but I leave it under the pillow, where I'm hiding it now. I reach under and it's still there, with the tip of the key still there too.

I had a good look at the key tonight. It's as long as my pointer finger, but flat. It's got three bumps cut in it at one end, and the other end is round, with a hole in it. There's writing on that end with a number stamped underneath—*Diebold*, it says, *158*. It's kinda yellowy gold and old-timey looking, like something somebody would take out of a vest pocket in a black–and-white movie. So that's what it looks like, but what it opens, I don't know. What I do know is that my hand would stop paining so bad if I could run some cold water on it— numb it up a bit. Which I do, by heading down to the bathroom, making sure Flarehead's not around before I go in. It's when I'm sneaking back from the bathroom that I hear the noise again—the crying. And this time I know it's Ribs.

"Hey," I whisper into his room. "Ribs—it's me, Charlie. You okay?"

More snorting like last night, except this time he can't stop crying.

"Hey, Ribs," I say, taking a couple of steps into the room. "How come you're crying? I won't tell anybody."

No answer, so I show my hand to him.

"Busted it up," I say.

"How?" he says after a bit.

"Squeezed it in the door—in the bathroom."

"Let's see."

I give him a closer look.

"Don't look like much," he says, leaning forward to squint in the moonlight.

"Hurts though."

"Yeah," says Ribs. "I've had plenty of stuff happen that hurts. But I weren't crying about anything like that."

"So why were you crying?"

"It's too stupid."

"I do some pretty stupid things—like squeezing my hand in the door."

Ribs lets out a little laugh that he kinda chokes on.

"Stupid, right?" I say.

"Well," says Ribs, "what I'm crying about is really stupid… you promise you won't tell nobody?"

"Promise."

"You know them *Harry Potter* movies?" he asks.

"Yeah."

"They showed us one a couple of weeks ago. It had a girl in it—I don't know how you say her name."

"Hermione…"

"Guess so," says Ribs. "She got a secret potion that turned her into somebody else."

"Polyjuice Potion. Where you take something from a person and drop it into a potion, and it turns you into that person."

Ribs sits up in his bed. "I tried making my own—to turn me into Billy, the van driver."

For the first time in about a month, I almost laugh. But I don't.

Ribs keeps going. "I don't know what she put in her potion—it don't say in the movie—so I tried using some Pepsi and a bit of his hair."

"Billy's hair?"

"Yeah. Off a his jacket. Just a little one. Dropped in the Pepsi, let it sit there for a day..."

"And you drank it?"

Ribs nods. "A bit last night, and the rest tonight. I felt a bit funny today, so I thought it might be starting to work, but I finished the last of it after light's out and nothing happened— I feels just the same as I always did."

He leans close to me. "Do I look any different?"

"Pretty much the same."

"Jesus," says Ribs, starting to cry again. "I got six weeks left in here—I gotta figure something out. If this don't work..."

He turns back to me. "Do you think stuff like that can work? Magic stuff?"

I sit there for a bit, thinking about what's right to say. 'cause the truth is I don't really believe in that stuff, in wizards and potions. I don't even believe in Santa Claus. Haven't for a long time, three years—four if you count the year I didn't really believe but really wanted to at the same time. Which is how I feel about a lot of things like magic and religion. I sorta want to believe it, but I don't.

Like in the hospital, when I was looking at my dad hooked up to all those wires. Right then, I shut my eyes real tight and squinted out a little prayer—not an official one, but a quick little one of my own, direct to God. Said my name, Charlie Sykes, and what I wanted—that my dad would be okay. Not even okay, I said after that, just that he'd live. And even when I was doing it, I thought, This isn't going to work. But right at the same time—the same instant—I tried to keep that thought away, buried down inside, so God wouldn't know I was thinking it. That's a complicated thing to do, to try and fool a God you don't think is out there into thinking you really believe in him.

What I was really doing was hoping. I was doing it again this morning, thinking about my mom maybe being alive. And Ribs, he's doing it too—hoping for a way to get himself outta here. But is it right to keep that hope going with a lie about pretend wizards who're going to solve all your problems with a wand?

"Is there...?" he asks again. "Is there some potion stuff I can use?"

I let out a big sigh. Jesus, I'm doing it now, the sighing.

"I don't...," I say, then start again. "I think a lot of the stuff in books is made up, and that it can't really happen—stuff like, I don't know, *Jack and the Beanstalk*."

"What's that?" says Ribs.

I look at him, but I can't tell in the dark if he's joking or not.

"You don't know *Jack and the Beanstalk*?"

"Was it a movie?"

"It's a story—an old story. What's a story you know?"

"I seen that *Charlie and the Chocolate Factory*."

"Okay. Like that. The movie shows rivers of chocolate and stuff, but you know there aren't really any rivers like that…"

"I guess not," says Ribs.

"So I kinda think that's the way it is with wizards and potions. They're good in a book, but I don't figure you should count on them to get you out of a place like this."

"Get out?" says Ribs, looking at me like I'm crazy. "It ain't getting out that I wants to do."

Then he's crying harder than ever, turning round to hide his face in the pillow.

Looking at him, so little, crying and shaking like that, it doesn't seem fair. I mean, what's a kid got waiting at home that makes him want to stay in a place like this? It makes me sorta angry, thinking about that. Ribs is even littler than me, younger than me, so what could he do that he deserves a home that's so bad he doesn't ever want to go back?

I put out my hand to give him a pat—just a little one. And it's only when I see it sitting there on his shoulder that I notice it's not hurting so much.

NINE

Next afternoon I meet Frankie again at the Catwalk, both of us on landscape duty. Soon as he sees me, he reaches into his jacket and pulls out a cardboard tube—the thing that goes in the middle of a roll of paper towel.

"Here," he says, putting it in my hand.

He sees my fingers are hurting when I take hold of it.

"What happened to your hand?" he says.

"Jammed it in a door."

"But you can still write, can't ya?"

"Yeah."

"Good. Test's in that—all rolled up, nice and clean. Just pull it out and fill it in. But don't go folding it—it's gotta look just like the one Aikens hands out. Got it?"

I nod.

"And take this too," he says, reaching in his jeans and pulling out a piece of loose-leaf. There's writing on it in blue pen: *Frankie Walsh, 119 Saunders Avenue, St. John's.*

"What's this?"

"My address," says Frankie. "It's about the only words I knows how to write. You study on it, then make your answers look like that. And don't do too good a job. Get a few wrong, leave a couple hard ones blank. Just get enough right to get me a pass."

"It still feels like it's cheating," I say.

"Not that shit again," says Frankie. And I can tell he's getting mad. "I told you—it's just doing right by me, after I done right by you."

"So once I do this, we're all even. And then maybe you can do something else for me."

Frankie gives a wink. "Right, b'y."

"I got a favor in mind," I say, but Frankie holds up his hand.

"Whoa, Cowboy. I don't want to hear it till I gets my pass. Once I gets that, we can talk about what happens next."

"Okay. When do you need this?"

"Test is tomorrow, second period, so I needs it at breakfast. Just do it up tonight and leave that tube on your breakfast tray. I'll be right there."

He lights up a smoke and grabs his rake.

"You stay here while I heads out front," he says. "And remember, don't be too smart. And use a pencil. And make it look like my writing. Okay?"

"'Kay," I say, leaning against the Catwalk rail as he heads off.

Once he's gone I look for the girl from yesterday. I been thinking about what I'll do if I see her—how I'll give her a nod and walk on up to the gate, real slow, and maybe say "Hey" when I get there.

And she's there now—or she's almost there, walking over the top of the hill, down toward the gate. Now that I see her, I kinda forget about my plans and feel like running away. But before I can move, she waves. At least I think it's a wave. She just sorta tosses her arm out and lets it fall. But I think it was a wave. I look round but there's no one else to wave to, so it musta been to me. Then she does it again, which means it's gotta be a wave. So I give a little wave myself, which, even when I'm doing it, I think is the stupidest wave ever—just a little floppy-arm wave that a two-year-old would do.

Then she does what I was going to do—nods her head, and again, the Come Over Here sign. I go over. And not as slow as I had been planning.

"Hey," she says when I get close. "You *can* see."

"Sure," I say. "I can see fine."

"I wasn't sure. I waved a couple of times and you just ignored me, so I thought maybe you were blind."

She pulls a hand across her face, like yesterday, to get her hair outta her eyes. A finger gets caught in some that's blown in between her lips. They're open in just a bit of a smile—a tiny smile like one you might smile on a Sunday, thinking about something fun you did on a Saturday.

She loops the hair behind her ear and puts her hands in her back pockets.

"But you're not, are you?" she says. "Blind?"

"No. I just thought maybe you were waving to somebody else."

"To your friend?"

"Yeah. To Frankie."

"Frankie," she says, like she's been wondering what his name was. "Frankie looks like a tough guy."

"Pretty tough."

"But I guess most of you guys over there are pretty tough."

"Pretty tough," I say. Again.

"Are you pretty tough?"

"Tough enough."

"Well, Tough Enough, I'm Estelle."

"That's a nice name."

"It is. That's why I tell people it's my name sometimes—just to hear it. But it's not really my name. I'm really Clare."

"That's nice too."

"I hate it," she says, and all of a sudden that little smile goes away.

"Anyway," Clare says, "what do they call you?"

"Charlie."

"Well, Charlie," she says, taking a hand outta her back pocket and putting three fingers through the chain link. "Nice to meet you."

I reach out and give them a quick shake. They're about the warmest thing I ever felt. I want to hold on longer but pull back, because it's hurting.

"Sore fingers?" she asks, seeing me wince.

"Yeah," I say. "Jammed 'em in a door."

"That hurts," she says. She's not looking at me anymore—instead she's looking off behind me, off to nowheres.

"Not as much as a burn hurts though," she says after a bit. "You ever have a burn?" she asks, looking back at me.

"Sure," I say. "I been burned a bunch of times." I say it to sound tough, but as soon as I say it, I figure it makes me sound stupid more than anything.

"Ever get one on purpose?" she asks.

"On purpose?"

I let out a little laugh at that, which, as soon as I do, I wish I hadn't.

"No. By accident."

"Some girls do it on purpose here. With cigarettes. Or they cut themselves."

I don't know what to say to that, so I don't say anything.

"You ever do that? Cut yourself?"

"Not on purpose. That what you mean?"

"That's what I mean. I don't either—it's just some of the girls here do. That's why some of them are here. But not me."

She wraps her arms around herself like she's cold, which she could be since the wind is blowing.

"What are you in for?" she says.

"I'm not really in."

She gives a laugh this time. "You're just visiting?"

"Sorta. I'm just staying here for a little bit."

"Because you're just a little bit bad?"

"'Cause I'm waiting for a foster home, and there's nowhere else to put me."

Clare gets ready to say something to that when a woman calls out from up the hill.

"Clare," she calls. "Clare Dalton. You know the rules."

Clare looks at me and gives her eyes a big roll. They're green, like the ocean some days.

"We're not supposed to talk to the boys," she says, turning round to walk up the hill to where the woman's standing. She stops after a couple of steps and looks back at me.

"But I do," she says, then turns back up the hill.

I watch Clare Dalton go till she's gone.

TEN

The test is easy—just some story about a fireman who puts out a fire. Then there are ten questions with multiple-choice answers. Stuff like, Who is the "I" in this story: A) the man whose house burns down, B) the fireman, or C) the firehouse dog. Pretty simple. I mean, how stupid would you have to be to pick C? But I guess if you couldn't read, maybe you'd just pick any old thing. Anyway, I could have done the whole thing in about one minute, except I had to concentrate on making my writing look like Frankie's. But that didn't take much time since I only had to write in his name and one little sentence at the end where it asks you to write about how you think the fireman feels after he puts out the fire. I said he felt happy, but then I thought maybe he wouldn't feel happy exactly, since the guy whose house burnt down lost a lot of his stuff, and it's probably not right to feel happy about something bad happening to someone else—even if you're helping them.

So I erased *happy* and wrote in *good*, which maybe is the same thing. I don't know. Is it?

Then I remembered I shouldn't get all the questions right, so I had to make a couple of them wrong, and that took more time than you might think. In the end I put down six right answers, left one blank and got three wrong, though I might only get two wrong, since number nine about who is the bravest guy in the story is a bit ambiguous. I figure the right answer is the fireman, but it could also be the guy who owns the house, since he doesn't cry or freak out or anything when his house is burning down, and he gets his wife and kids out okay before the fire truck even shows up. So he's pretty brave, I think. And the fireman is only doing what he gets paid to do.

I like that word, *ambiguous*. It's Latin, like a lot of words are. *Ambi*—that's the root—it means "both ways." I read that in a dictionary, which is something I like to read every once in a while. Really, I do. First time I read one was at school with Robert, and I only read it because he told me it had swear words in it. I didn't believe him until he showed me *fuck*, right there between *fuchsite* and *fucoid*. So right away Robert wanted to look up a bunch of other words, like *prick* and *tits*, and they were there, too, right there in this big old *Shorter Oxford Dictionary*—which isn't very short—sitting in the middle of the library at school, looking all respectable and heavy and full of words you'd get expelled for saying in class. Robert kept wanting to look up more dirty words, but I wanted to look up *fuchsite*, which is a green chromium-containing variety of muscovite. But who knows what muscovite is?

So I look that up, and it's a potassium-containing mica, which I also had to look up. That's how it is with a dictionary—once you start looking up one word, you gotta look up another one and another one—like eating chips, but with your mind.

Only trouble was, after Robert told everybody about the words in there, a couple of kids started saying them to the teachers, and when the teachers got mad, the kids would say, "I learned 'em in the dictionary." One kid even said it to the principal.

Not long after that, the big old dictionary turned up gone, and a new one took its place. It had a picture of a jet on the front and no dirty words inside. Some note got sent home to parents about it. And my dad, he went out and bought me a big dictionary for myself, even though it wasn't my birthday or anything.

"You look up whatever words you want," he told me. "It's good to know what things mean. Makes it tougher for people to trick you."

Truth is, I'll read about anything—even stuff I won't ever do, like how to gap a spark plug or how to make Rice Krispies squares. I just like reading. So this test of Frankie's would have only taken me two minutes except for all the stuff I had to think about. Anyway, I got it finished and shoved it back inside the tube just before lights-out. Then I thought about Clare for a bit, how her fingers felt when I touched them, how she asked about my hand. Then I fell asleep.

This morning at breakfast everything went like Frankie said. I left the roll on my tray and Frankie got it without anybody noticing. I didn't see him again until lunch, out at the Catwalk. Soon as he saw me come round the corner, he held out the test, a big smile on his face.

"Six outta ten," he says, slapping me on the back. "This is my ticket outta here, thanks to you."

I take the test from him and look at number nine, about the hero. I chose the guy whose house burned down, which is marked wrong.

"We're even now?" I say, handing it back.

"Even."

"So…," I say.

"So I owes you one," says Frankie. "Ask away."

"It's not that big a favor. It's just I'm wondering if you know anything about my family—my dad and his brother."

"You don't know nothing about Nick Sykes?" says Frankie. He's squinting at me, and not because there's smoke in his eyes.

"I didn't even know my dad had a brother till last week."

"Like shit."

"It's true. He never told me about his brother, or his mom and dad, or anybody. Honest."

Frankie looks at me a good long while.

"So how'd you know about 'em now?"

"From some guy with Child Services. Dez somebody—"

"Dezzy boy," says Frankie. "And what did Dezzy boy have to say about Nick Sykes? Nothing good, I'm guessing."

"Nothing good or bad. Just that he couldn't look after me right now, but that maybe some old aunt might be able to."

"I don't know nothing about any old aunt," says Frankie. "But I guess he's right about Nick not being able to take you in."

"How come?"

"'Cause he's inside. Locked up."

"In prison?"

Frankie nods.

"What'd he do?"

Frankie puts his face in his hands to light up a smoke.

"Murder," he says in a puff.

"He killed somebody?"

"Two somebodies."

"My uncle? Killed two people?"

"That they know about," says Frankie. "It was a long time ago—'fore I were born. I only knows about it 'cause the old man used to talk about the Sykes when he were drinking—telling stories about how they was the baddest family on the island, how everything that got stole from St. John's to Corner Brook went through them 'fore it got shipped off to the mainland. Cops could never catch 'em, he said, 'cause they had these secret hideaways and bank accounts all over the place where they stashed their loot. But it weren't the cops what got 'em in the end anyways."

"What was it?"

"Fire," says Frankie. "One night. Winter. Burned down a whole row of places up on Cook Street. Three or four people killed, 'cluding Dick and Doreen Sykes."

"My grandparents," I say.

"After that, your old man and his brother—Mikey and Nick—they got shipped off up to Cliffside."

"Cliffside?"

"The orphanage—run by the Brothers. You never heard a that neither?"

I shake my head.

"Jesus, Cowboy," says Frankie. "For a smart kid, you don't know so much."

"How I am supposed to know about some orphanage in Newfoundland, all the way out in Alberta?"

"Sure, it was all over the news—'bout how them pervert brothers abused the orphans, felt 'em up, screwed 'em, all that shit. You never heard about any of that?"

"I heard about stuff and the Indians, 'bout when they put them in those schools."

"This was kind of like that, only worse," says Frankie, "'cause them little bastards up at Cliffside didn't have no one to even tell about it."

"And my dad was in that place?"

"Yeah," says Frankie. "I don't know no details—just what the old man told me when he was cursing out the church. I know, for sure, though, that Nick was in there, 'cause that's where he killed the Brother."

"He killed a priest?"

"Them queers weren't priests, exactly. They called 'em Brothers—kind of like monks, not allowed to get married and stuff. And Nicky killed one of 'em—some guy who was messin' with him."

I'm breathing fast now, little breaths that don't go down into my lungs. I sit on the ground.

"Jesus, Cowboy," says Frankie. "Don't go fainting on me. This is old stuff happened, like, twenty years ago."

"And my dad," I say, looking up at Frankie. "Did he...?"

Frankie shakes his head. "He never killed nobody—nobody I ever heard about. I don't really know. It's all just drunk talk from my old man."

I put my head between my knees and take a couple a deep breaths to make things stop spinning.

"I gotta find out," I say.

"Find out what?"

"'Bout my dad—my uncle—what happened at that place."

A thought hits me. "Is it still open?"

"What?"

"The orphanage—Cliffside—is it still open?"

I'm shouting loud enough that Frankie holds out his hand, waving me to be quiet.

"Jesus, Cowboy. Stop freaking out, will ya? It's been closed for years, b'y."

Then his face gets soft and he bends down to look at me.

"They can't put you in there, Cowboy," he says, quiet like. "It's tore down, crushed up and hauled away. You ain't going there."

I'm crying but I can't help it—I don't care if Frankie sees me. It's like something's pulling at me, in a part of my chest I never knew I had. Frankie lets me cry for a bit, then pulls out another smoke.

"Want one now?"

"No," I say. I take a big snort in and wipe my cheeks off.

"I didn't mean to get you crying," says Frankie.

"It's okay."

I take another big snort.

"Do you think…?"

I want to ask a question—another question I'm not sure if I want to know the answer to. But this one, I gotta ask.

"Do you think those Brothers—do you think they did anything to my dad?"

"I don't know, Cowboy."

"Maybe your dad—maybe he might know."

Frankie shakes his head.

"Naw. You don't want to be asking my dad about nothing. Trust me."

"But I gotta know."

"Guess you could google it—do one a them searches on your old man and Nicky."

"Maybe," I say.

"'Cept you can't do one here—they yanked the computers last winter. Too much por-no-gra-phy."

He gives me that sly smile.

"But the girls still got them, on the other side. Maybe you could get your girlfriend to help you—the one you was talking to yesterday."

He gives a nod up the hill, toward the gate, and there's Clare standing behind it.

"Worth a try," he says and starts walking round the front. But not before he takes a good long look up at Clare, with that sly smile on his face the whole time. Right then, I don't like him, and I don't like him even more 'cause I can't do anything about it.

Soon as he leaves, I give my face another wipe and head up toward the gate.

"Hey, Tough Enough," she says when I get close. "You two looked pretty intense down there."

"Yeah," I say. "Listen, I got a favor to ask."

"Okay."

"You guys got computers over there—ones you can do a search on?"

Clare nods. "Some stuff's blocked though. YouTube, medical stuff. Porn."

"What about newspapers? Can you search those?"

"I think so. I don't use it much, just to check email—and even that has to go through the office server. Don't want us setting up drug deals."

I look to see if she's kidding, but she's not smiling.

"So if I give you some names, you could google them?"

"Sure. Who?"

"There's two. Michael Sykes and Nick Sykes."

"Okay. Michael and Nick Sykes. S-y-k-e-s?"

I nod.

"Okay. I'll do it this afternoon…How's your hand?"

"It's okay. Looks worse, but hurts less."

I show the bruise to her.

"I'll go do that search now," Clare says. "And see you out here tomorrow."

I nod again.

"Say hi to Frankie from me."

"Sure," I say, but she's already headed back up the hill. Watching her go, I think maybe I won't say anything to Frankie at all.

ELEVEN

Soon as I see Clare the next day, I know she's read the stuff and that it isn't good.

"Hey, Charlie," Clare says when I get to the fence.

"Hey."

"This is from the search."

She slips a bunch of papers through the fence.

"Sorry about your dad—there's a story about the accident in there."

"You read it?"

"Sure. You didn't say not to."

"Guess not."

"There's other stuff too—about your uncle."

"'Bout him killing people?"

She nods.

All of a sudden I'm almost crying.

"I gotta go—gotta read this," I say, turning to head back to The Hollow.

"See you tomorrow," Clare calls out, but I don't turn round. Instead I go right to my room, shut the door and start reading.

The Telegram, Monday, May 15, 1989

POLICE SEEK MAN IN CONNECTION WITH MURDER

Police started a province-wide search over the weekend for Nick Sykes, a St. John's man suspected of killing a member of the Brothers of the Holy Order Saturday evening.

Officers from the Royal Newfoundland Constabulary and the RCMP manned checkpoints at the airport in St. John's and at the Port aux Basques ferry terminal to the mainland after issuing a country-wide arrest warrant for Sykes on Sunday.

He's wanted in the death of Brother Sean Sullivan, 53, who was found dead Saturday evening in his apartment at the Cliffside Orphanage in St. John's. The orphanage is run by the Brothers of the Holy Order.

Sykes had been a resident of the orphanage since 1987 and left last year when he turned eighteen.

Several Brothers at the orphanage are being investigated for alleged physical and sexual abuse of boys there over the past two decades, although police say Br. Sullivan is not among them.

RNC Staff Sgt. Randy Turpin says witness reports led them to issue the warrant against Sykes, though he wouldn't give details on what witnesses told police.

Sykes is a white male, 19, with dark curly hair and a medium build. When last seen he was wearing blue jeans, a brown leather jacket and work boots.

Police say anyone spotting him should contact them immediately. They cautioned against approaching him, describing him as dangerous and possibly armed.

The Telegram, Tuesday, May 16, 1989

SYKES STILL AT LARGE

Police continued their search yesterday for the man wanted in connection with the murder of a Brother of the Holy Order in St. John's over the weekend.

A warrant was issued Sunday for the arrest of Nick Sykes, 19, just hours after the body of Brother Sean Sullivan was discovered in Sullivan's apartment at the Cliffside Orphanage Saturday evening.

Police are releasing a few more details about what they believe happened that night, noting witnesses describe hearing an altercation between Sullivan and Sykes early Saturday evening.

Sykes was seen leaving the orphanage just after six that evening.

An appeal for the public's help in locating Sykes brought in several sightings over the past 24 hours, says RNC Staff Sgt. Randy Turpin.

"We've had a few good reports, all of which we've looked into," Turpin said Monday. "There's been a cluster down toward Trepassey, but nothing substantial yet."

The public is warned not to approach Sykes, but rather to contact police.

Sykes is a white male, 19, with dark curly hair and a medium build. When last seen, he was wearing blue jeans and work boots. He was also wearing a brown jacket, which police now describe as vinyl, not leather, as reported Monday.

The Telegram, Thursday, May 18, 1989

SYKES ARRESTED IN TREPASSEY

Police arrested murder suspect Nick Sykes yesterday without a struggle after a postal worker reported seeing him leaving the Trepassey post office shortly after noon Wednesday.

Sykes is wanted for the killing of Brother Sean Sullivan, who was slain Saturday in St. John's.

The tip that led police to Sykes came from an unidentified worker at the post office who saw the suspect leaving the building just as she returned from a lunch break.

Police believe he was searching the post office for cash since he had no money on his person when he was arrested.

Sykes will appear in court today.

The Telegram, Friday, May 19, 1989

File not found, contact server

The Telegram, Tuesday, September 12, 1989

WITNESS PUTS SYKES AT SCENE

Nick Sykes's first-degree murder trial began Monday in St. John's with a young witness putting Sykes at the scene of the murder just hours before Sean Sullivan's body was found last May.

The witness, whose identity is protected due to his age, was a resident of the Cliffside Orphanage at the time of the murder.

Under questioning by Crown Prosecutor Francine Richards, the witness told Judge Nelson Hamilton that he heard raised voices inside Sullivan's apartment around suppertime on Saturday, May 13.

He told the judge he couldn't identify who was speaking, only that they seemed to be having a heated disagreement "with lots of yelling."

The witness testified the argument was still going on when he went to supper, just before 5:30 PM. He headed back to his room shortly after 6:00, but went outside the orphanage briefly to search for a jacket he'd left at the playground earlier in the day. He testified that as he was getting his jacket, he saw someone leaving Brother Sullivan's apartment through a rear window that exits onto a fire escape. He identified that person as Nick Sykes.

Testimony later in the day from RNC specialist Norm Henneberry showed police found footprints in the mud beneath the fire escape that matched the boots worn by Sykes when he was arrested three days later in Trepassey.

Henneberry testified the footprints were fresh and deep, consistent with an impression made by someone jumping from a height of several feet. The fire-escape ladder ends three feet, two inches above the ground, he told Judge Hamilton.

The trial continues today.

The Telegram, Wednesday, September 13, 1989

SYKES BROTHER REVEALS ABUSE

In a surprise move, the brother of suspected murderer Nick Sykes took the stand for the prosecution Tuesday, telling court Nick Sykes had made allegations of abuse against the Brother of the Holy Order he's accused of killing.

Michael Sykes, 17, told Judge Nelson Hamilton that Nick first mentioned the abuse when both Sykeses were living at the orphanage, in 1987.

"He said something happened with Brother Sullivan—nothing more than that at first," said Michael Sykes, who appeared nervous on the stand, frequently looking at his older brother.

The younger Sykes testified Nick eventually told him Sullivan had made "overtures of a sexual nature."

Asked for details about the "overtures" by Crown Prosecutor Francine Riche, Michael said his brother refused to discuss specific acts.

"He just said it made him feel dirty—that Brother Sullivan was a pervert."

Under cross-examination by defense lawyer Jerry Purdy, Michael admitted Nick never directly threatened revenge against Br. Sullivan.

"He just said it wasn't right—what was happening to the boys there—and that somebody ought to do something to make it stop," Michael testified.

Mr. Purdy then asked Michael if he believed Nick was referring to himself when he used the word *somebody*.

"I don't know who he meant," he told the court. "The police, the church, Child Services—just somebody had to stand up and do something to stop it. He told me nobody gave a damn what happened to us, because we wasn't rich kids—people figured we was just bad kids getting what we deserved."

The day's testimony took a toll on both brothers.

Michael appeared to be on the verge of crying more than once as he testified against his brother, while Nick used profanity in several shouted attacks where he denied what his brother was telling the court.

In the last and loudest attack, Nick warned his brother he'd never forgive him "for being a rat," telling Michael "you'll get what's coming" as sheriffs escorted him from the courtroom.

The two came face-to-face briefly when Nick Sykes was escorted to the prison van by sheriffs at the end of the day's testimony. Spotting Michael on the sidewalk, he lunged for his brother and had to be restrained by guards, who tore the elder Sykes's jacket in the altercation. The confrontation ended with Nick Sykes spitting into his brother's face before being dragged into the van.

Tuesday's testimony marks the first time the prosecution has entered evidence suggesting a

motive for the slaying. Police had earlier ruled out
robbery, since nothing was removed from Sullivan's
apartment.

Several Brothers at the orphanage are under
investigation for physical and sexual assaults against
boys there that extend back two decades, but until
Tuesday's testimony there had been no suggestion of
any abuse on the part of Brother Sullivan. The trial
continues tomorrow.

The Telegram, Thursday, September 14, 1989

File incomplete, error 177...determined the blow as
the cause of death.

"It fractured the victim's skull," testified Dr.
Wasabi.

"In this case," the pathologist said, "it appears the
single blow from a sharp object was sufficient to kill
the victim. The killer would have to have been in a
highly agitated state to deliver such a blow."

The Telegram, Monday, September 18, 1989

SYKES FOUND GUILTY
The jury hearing the case against Nick Sykes took
less than three hours to reach their verdict Saturday,

finding the St. John's man guilty of killing Brother Sean Sullivan last May.

But in returning a verdict of manslaughter rather than first-degree murder, the jury dismissed the Crown's closing argument that Sykes planned the killing in advance.

Still, the jury left no doubt that the 19-year-old was the person who battered Sullivan's skull inside the Brother's Cliffside Orphanage apartment, sometime between 5:00 and 6:00 PM on May 13.

Nick Sykes had lived at the orphanage between 1987 and 1988, when he was released at age 18. Also living there was his younger brother Michael, whose testimony for the prosecution last week established motive for the murder.

Sentencing will take place September 27.

The Telegram, Thursday, September 28, 1989

SYKES RECEIVES MINIMUM SENTENCE

Nick Sykes will spend the next 5 years inside a federal prison for killing Brother Sean Sullivan.

Judge Nelson Hamilton imposed the sentence Wednesday, rejecting the Crown's call for a sentence of at least 10 years.

"While causing the death of another human being is always a grave act," said the judge, "I had to take into account Nicholas Sykes's motivation for his attack stemmed from his own suffering at the hands of Brother Sullivan. While not excusing the attack, it does offer an insight into the workings of the attacker's mind."

Sykes was found guilty of manslaughter by a jury this month in the May slaying of Brother Sullivan.

Sykes's sentence will be served at the federal penitentiary in Dorchester, New Brunswick.

It began immediately, with the convicted murderer escorted from the courtroom in shackles, led away by two sheriff's officers.

The Telegram, Friday, August 2, 1993

SYKES KILLS AGAIN

Convicted killer Nick Sykes has been found guilty of second-degree murder in the death of a fellow inmate at the Dorchester Penitentiary in New Brunswick.

Sykes was found guilty Thursday, along with two other prisoners, who all took part in a March 14 riot that left one inmate dead and 13 injured. Three guards were also hospitalized after the riot, which began when an Easter showing of the movie *Ben Hur* was cancelled due to the discovery of illegal home-brewed liquor in several cells.

Sykes was convicted of murder along with Stephen Duchy and Art Griswald. New Brunswick

Supreme Court Justice Paul Caseman found all three equally responsible for planning and starting the fire on the prison's D Wing, which led to the death of a prisoner trapped in his cell.

A forensic fire specialist estimated temperatures in the cement-block cell approached 1,000°F, before its contents flashed over into a fierce blaze that burned for more than two hours.

In delivering his verdict, Justice Caseman noted, "The victim essentially cooked in his cell—a crueler death would be difficult to imagine."

Sykes suffered severe burns to his right hand in the blaze, which he and the co-accused started using contraband lighter fluid. The fluid was eventually traced to Sykes's cell. Sykes maintained his was burned in an attempt to pry open the locked cell door, though he had a long history of altercations with the deceased prisoner.

Sykes is in Dorchester, serving five years for the 1989 manslaughter death of Brother Sean Sullivan.

The Telegram, Monday, August 17, 2009

SYKES RETURNS TO ISLAND

Twice-convicted killer Nick Sykes has been transferred from Dorchester Penitentiary in New Brunswick to Her Majesty's Prison in St. John's as he prepares for mandatory release later this month.

Sykes was convicted of manslaughter in the death of Sean Sullivan in 1989. While in prison he was found guilty of second-degree murder for causing the death of a fellow prisoner during a riot in March 1993.

Both sentences will have expired on Friday, August 21.

There's no word on where Sykes plans to live.

The Telegram, Thursday, August 20, 2009

ACCIDENT VICTIM NAMED

Police have released the name of the man killed Wednesday when his vehicle struck a moose just before midnight on the Trans-Canada Highway near St. John's.

Michael Sykes died in hospital just hours after the collision, without regaining consciousness. The accident happened about 11:30 PM, near the Outer Ring Road on the city outskirts.

Sykes's 13-year-old son was in the car at the time but was not seriously injured. Police say he was orphaned in the accident and has been taken into care by the Newfoundland and Labrador Department of Child Services while arrangements for his long-term care are finalized.

I feel sick when I finish reading—not like I'm going to throw up, but crampy. I have to get to the toilet. One stall is locked, but I make it to the other one just in time, my insides like water. Finally I get up and wash my hands. I stand kinda sideways to the sink now when I wash my hands, to keep an eye on the door. It opens, but it's not Flarehead—it's Frankie, with a big smile on his face.

"Cowboy, my man," he says, stopping when he gets a closer look at me. "Jesus—you look like crap."

"Just sick. I'll be okay."

He gives a nod like he doesn't quite believe me, then says, "I thought I should tell ya—I'm getting sprung tomorrow."

"You're going home?"

"Don't know about home, but outta this shithole for sure. Van leaves at nine AM. By this time tomorrow, I'll be having a beer and talking some shit with the b'ys."

"That's good," I say, which I don't really mean.

He can tell I'm not too excited for him, because I'm sorta smiling one of those smiles you put on when you're pretty much trying not to cry.

"Listen, things'll work out. You'll be outta here in a couple a weeks and set up with some nice family out in Mount Pearl, with a big-screen TV in the rec room. I been in a couple a foster homes and some of them is pretty nice—Doritos and stuff anytime you wants 'em, let you stay up late watching the satellite. You'll see."

"I guess."

"And don't worry about Flarehead—I'll have a talk with him before I leaves."

Then he's out the door, and I'm looking down at the hand that Flarehead squashed. It doesn't really hurt much anymore, unless you squeeze the knuckles together. There's still some tenderness.

Then *bang!* Lights flash in the back of my eyes and my mouth fills up with the taste of old pennies that drip red onto my shirtfront from where my teeth bite into my tongue. I spit more blood into the sink and see Flarehead in the mirror—he must've come outta the other stall. Before I can move, he jumps on me, dropping me onto the floor, all two hundred pounds of him sitting right on my chest. I can't move. His breath stinks when he sticks his face close to mine.

"Your buddy's gonna talk to me, is he?" he says, all quiet so no one comes running to see what's happening. I try to yell, but Flarehead's so heavy on my chest I can't draw in any air.

"Gonna scream, are ya?" he says, feeling me trying to suck in air. He reaches over to the trash can by the sink and grabs a handful of old paper towels from inside. He shoves a wad of it, all wet and cardboardy, into my mouth.

"Try screaming now, you little shit," he says, but I can't scream or call out or breathe. I can't do anything—can't move my arms or legs. I figure I'm going to pass out when all of sudden Flarehead pulls himself off me and stands up, panting.

"That's a taste, Puke Pants," he says, shaking his fat fist down at me. "Come tomorrow, once your buddy's gone, it'll be ten times worse."

He takes one last kick at me, then walks out the door.

I yank the paper towel outta my mouth, strings of red spit hanging off it, then stick my head in the sink and gag. There's nothing there except blood and some yellow stuff. I let out a stinky burp and spit.

"Jesus," comes a voice from another person I don't see till he's right on top of me. I gotta get better at looking out for people. This time it's Pillsbury.

"What happened to you?" he says, looking down at the pile of blood and paper and garbage.

I almost laugh—really, I do—because just for a sec I get this picture in my mind like I'm looking down from up on the ceiling, down at me and Pillsbury and the blood in the sink and on my shirt, and the garbage all over the floor, and the air stinking of puke and crap, and I think, what's a good answer to "What happened to you?"

"Nothing," I say, leaving it up to Pillsbury to figure out how good an answer that is. Does he really care what happened? Or is he scared to know what happened? I look at him looking at me, and wait. His eyes do a couple a circles, taking it all in. The crap, my face, my shirt.

"Okay," he says.

Which makes me sad and happy, right at the same time. Sad, because I think that if anything like this ever happened to me before—if someone turned a corner and found me puking up blood in a sink, with garbage all around me—they would definitely not be okay with "Nothing" for an answer. No matter who it was—my dad or a teacher or a babysitter or a friend—they would think, Well, something happened. They'd care enough about me to think something happened. Now, nobody cares.

And that's the same thing that makes me happy. As soon as I realize that nobody cares, I get this picture in my mind of a bird flying up in the sky. Which is a funny thing to think of when you've just been smacked in the head and have puked your guts up in some crappy bathroom. But I think of it. And I feel like that bird. Not attached to anything. Free.

I keep feeling it when I bend down to pick up the paper towel, and put it back in the trash can. When I spit out the last of the blood and give the sink another rinse. When I wiggle my front teeth to make sure they're in there good and tight. I think it when I head for the door and go past Pillsbury, who's still looking at me but saying nothing. Which is okay now, because that's what happened here. Nothing. Except that I figured out I am not gonna stay in The Hollow to get the crap beat outta me by some crazy bully. I'm not gonna go live with some aunt whose nephew bashes people's heads in and burns them up. I'm not gonna go live with somebody in some place called Mount Pearl—even if they do have Doritos and satellite TV. I am not doing those things.

What I am doing is getting outta here. I don't know how or to where, but I know I'm going. I'm going and I'll be free. And nobody'll care.

TWELVE

That night at lights-out I shove all my stuff in my backpack—my jeans, my underwear and socks, the Oilers T-shirt. I've got my wallet, too, and the money my dad gave me for this trip, except for $3.12 I spent in North Sydney on a chocolate bar and a pop. The key I take outta the Bible and put under the insole in my sneaker. The Bible I put back in the desk. I am gonna be ready to get outta here when there's a chance. Maybe tomorrow or the next day I'll grab my pack and sneak out when everybody is doing yard work. Or maybe I'll walk out through the main gate and nobody'll notice. Then, after a week or two, not a person in the world will even remember Charlie Sykes, and I can head back to Alberta—maybe hang out at Robert's place for a bit. I don't know. What I do know is I'm taking off soon as I get the chance. And nobody'll care.

Well, maybe Clare would, for a bit, but after a day or two she'd just figure I got sent to a foster home. Miz—she'd wonder where I was because it's her job to know where I am, but after a month she'd just take my files outta her big black bag and she'd put 'em in a big black filing cabinet, and after a year they'd end up at the back of the filing cabinet. And nobody would think of me again, except maybe once in a while, just long enough to wonder whatever happened to that kid from Alberta whose dad got killed in that car accident.

I pull my backpack out from under the bed and put it right beside me, just in case I feel like making a break for it if I wake up at 3:30 or some stupid time like that. I put my arm around the pack and it feels nice—even if it sounds stupid. Having something else in bed with you is nice. Like, sometimes my dad, when he'd get home real late from a shift, he'd come in and lay down beside me, smelling of beer and cigarettes. But I didn't mind, because it was nice if I woke up in the night to hear him breathing there beside me, all quiet, not angry or sad or anything. I think of that, trying to fall asleep. How good that felt.

In the morning I'm still holding that backpack, which is what Frankie sees when he comes through the door.

"Jesus," he says, laughing. "Get a girl, will ya?"

I'm too tired to even care what he's talking about.

"C'mon, b'y—time you was up. Almost gone eight."

He gives the bed a kick.

"Anyways," he says, "I just come in to say see ya. I'm getting the van into town in a couple a minutes."

"No, you're not," comes a voice. It's Billy, the driver.

"Van's been delayed, Walsh. And you, Sykes, you need to get your arse outta that bed and up to the superintendent's office right now. C'mon. Let's go."

Five minutes later, me and Billy are both sat down in the office, Mr. Delaney looking real serious.

"Charlie," he says, "bit of news for you. Yesterday, the medical examiner's office released your father's remains, so there's to be a small service today."

"Today?"

Mr. Delaney nods. "This morning, in fact. In about ninety minutes."

"You mean a funeral?"

"A service," says Mr. Delaney. "Dez Fitzpatrick will explain it to you in more detail. He's going to meet you at the funeral home in St. John's. You remember Mr. Fitzpatrick from Child Services? That's why the bus has been delayed—you'll ride in with Billy here, and he'll drop you at the funeral home."

"For a funeral?" I say again. "With a coffin and stuff?"

"Not exactly a funeral," Mr. Delaney says. "More a memorial service."

"What's the difference?"

There's a long pause before Billy pipes in.

"There's no body," Billy says.

Mr. Delaney groans. "Billy—it might be more appropriate for Mr. Fitzpatrick to speak to Charlie about this."

"What do you mean 'no body'?" I say. "I thought you just said they were giving away the body."

"Releasing it," says Mr. Delaney. "That's true—they authorized the release of your father's remains. But since there was no family member in a position to...to..."

"Pay," says Billy. He has a little grin on when he says it.

"To *authorize* a funeral," says Mr. Delaney. "The province had the body cremated."

"Burned up? My dad's been burned up?"

"Cremated," says Mr. Delaney, looking at me like a teacher trying to explain how come there's an X in a math equation.

"Yeah," I say, "I know—burned up."

I'm mad—mad that nobody even talked to me about any of this before they went ahead and did it. And now it's too late, because of all the things in the world that you can do and sorta change around if somebody doesn't like it, burning up a body isn't one of them. I mean, once it's burned, it's gone—into ashes. Right then I get a picture in my mind of the crinkled-up black newspaper my dad used to start a fire the time we went camping up north. And that's my dad now. Ashes. And what are ashes? Something that can only ever get smaller and smaller each time you touch them, until they're not there at all. Till they disappear. Which is what they've done to my dad, without even telling me about it till after it was done. Made him disappear.

"That's not right," I say. "To do that, without even telling me."

"It wouldn't have made any difference, Charlie," says Mr. Delaney. "You're a minor—under sixteen. The province made the decision for you."

"But that's not right. Somebody I don't even know—some guy who never even met my dad—decides he's going to get cremated like that."

"But that's how it is."

"But it's not right."

"Well," Mr. Delaney says, "somebody has to make those kinds of decisions. I mean, we can't have thirteen-year-old boys off wandering around the streets, making their own decisions about things, about where they'll live or how they'll get food. We'd end up with beggar children, like Calcutta or something."

"At least in Calcutta, if they're going to burn somebody up, they figure it's going to send the person to heaven or some-wheres," I say.

I know a little bit about India, because I saw a show once about how they make these pyres and wrap up bodies and burn them, then put the ashes in the river and float them off to God. Which, when you think about it, is no more of a crazy way to send somebody to heaven than sticking them in a big box in the ground. Try getting outta that—a big box under six feet of mud. I'd rather end up floating down a river any day.

"Look," says Mr. Delaney with that voice grown-ups get when they decide they're not going to talk about something anymore, "I understand you're upset, but I'm not going to discuss government policy with you."

He looks up at Billy and says to him, like I'm not even there, "God, this isn't even my job."

He turns back to me. "Dez Fitzpatrick will tell you all about this—why it happened and so forth."

"Can I at least get my backpack before I go?" I say. "It's got my Bible in it, and a good shirt."

Mr. Delaney shrugs. "Sure, get your backpack. Then meet Billy at the van."

I head to Brookside to grab my pack and have a last look round. I check all the closets for the fiftieth time since last night to make sure I'm not leaving anything behind, but they're empty, like I know they will be. Then I'm in the doorway, with one look back. And it's funny, but I don't feel anything except happy that I won't ever see this room again. Usually I feel a little sad leaving a place, even a place where I only lived for a while—like the apartment on Quarry Road that smelled like cat pee. Even though it did stink, I liked the way the sun came through the bedroom window after school, and how it made a bright patch on the brick building in the backyard. Except it did stink, and my dad was happy to get outta there. But I was a bit sad, closing that door for the last time.

Not now. I'm just happy. Which is a funny thing to be when you just heard your dad has been cremated. I think about that when I get into the van. I decide maybe cremation's not such a bad thing. I mean, my dad is dead—it isn't like he was gonna come back. Maybe it is better to be burned up into ash than to get put in a coffin and stuffed underground, where worms and beetles and sow bugs can get at you. Let's face it, no matter how much money you spend on a fancy coffin, they're gonna get in eventually. So maybe getting cremated isn't so bad after all. That's what I'm thinking when Frankie hops into the van and smacks me on the back.

"Cowboy," he says, "didn't know you was getting sprung too."

"I'm not. I'm going to a service for my dad. They cremated him."

"I thought he was dead," says Frankie.

"He is dead. But they cremated him—burned up his body."

Frankie gives his head a slow tilt back, like he's just hearing what I said.

"Oh, yeah," he says. "Cremated, right."

I nod.

"And they burned up his body?" he says.

I nod again.

"That's where they, like, toss your ashes around after, right? Throw 'em in the field where you first got laid, or fling 'em in the ocean."

"I guess."

"So what are you gonna do with your old man's?"

"I don't know. They never told me about doing anything like that."

"Me, I'd give the old man a burial at sea. Dump them ashes straight into the toilet, then flush 'em out to the harbor, along with all the other shit that ends up down there."

Billy sticks his head in through the front screen.

"Sykes, Charlie," he calls.

"Here," I say.

"Walsh, Frankie."

"Present," he says. "For another half hour."

"Oh, you'll be back, Walsh," Billy says.

"Nope," says Frankie. "I turns eighteen next month."

"Lucky us," says Billy. "It'll be Her Majesty's Penitentiary for you next time."

"No next time," says Frankie. "I'm a readin', writin', reformed character. Goin' straight."

"Straight to the Pen," says Billy, before he puts the van in gear and heads down the driveway. We swing round a bend, and I get a look at the Catwalk along the back of the school. It's just the fence and the gate at the top, with no one standing there. I look hard, but there's still no one, and just for a second I get that old feeling like when I close a door for the last time.

THIRTEEN

Frankie doesn't say anything for a while, just stares out the window. Blobs of rain drag across the glass, leaving little trails behind them. They look like snails, a whole herd of them, headed for the back of the van. Though you probably don't call a bunch of snails a herd. And they probably don't move anywhere in a bunch. But who knows with snails? Some scientist, probably. I bet there's a scientist out there who's spent his life studying snails—how they move around, how they have sex. Because scientists are always thinking about how stuff has sex. Which makes me feel better, because lately I am too. For a while I was worried I might be a bit crazy, with all this sex stuff popping into my head—like even when I'm thinking of snails. But it happens to scientists too. And they're pretty normal.

What's Frankie thinking about, I wonder? He's just staring out the window, looking at trees—I guess they're trees, all blown over and tiny. When Dad told me we were coming to Newfoundland, I got a picture in my mind of waves and oceans and seagulls, but so far it's been brick buildings and highways and florescent lights. And all these scrubby little trees, blown around by the wind. Not much ocean, except for what we crossed on the boat, and I was asleep for most of that.

"I loves this," Frankie says. He turns toward me.

"What?"

"This feeling I'm feeling—the feeling I gets when I leaves The Hollow."

"Going home, you mean?"

"Home?" says Frankie. He gives a snort. "Forget home. No, I mean…I don't know, just this…being out, you know? Like in the spring, and the snow melts, and you can walk on the sidewalk instead of halfways out in the road, and you can just stick your hands in your pockets and walk, and you got twenty bucks in your hand and a buddy who's gonna buy some beers and it's warm enough to sit out. It's like that, the feeling."

I'm not exactly sure what he means. I think I know. I think it's like the feeling you get the first day you can walk to school in your sneakers instead of your snow boots. But maybe that's not what he means. So I don't say anything.

"You don't know what it's like to get sprung, do you, Cowboy? 'Cause you never been inside—not really inside."

"Guess not."

"So what do you think about it—being inside?"

"Not much."

"Food's the best bit," says Frankie. "Having it regular."

I nod.

"And the worst," Frankie says, with the grown-up grin, "is being off the beer—and the pussy."

I look at the seat back in front of me when he says that.

"Course you're too young for the beer," he say, giving me a poke. "C'mon, Cowboy. Give us a laugh."

"The worst part for me," I say, "was my dad getting killed. And Flarehead."

"Yeah," Frankie says. "I knows you liked your old man. That's tough. Flarehead though—don't worry 'bout him. I gave him a talking to before I left."

"I'm not worried."

Frankie's face scrinches up for a sec, like he's surprised. "That's good," he says.

"I'm not going to see him again."

"'Cause ya got a foster home?"

"'Cause I'm not going back."

"Whaddaya mean you're not going back?"

"I'm not going back," I say.

"But ya don't got a foster home?"

I shake my head.

"So a Sykes is taking ya in?"

"No."

"So what are you sayin', Cowboy?"

"I'm saying I'm not going back to The Hollow."

Frankie sits up straight to have a good look at Billy, who's got his eyes on the road and the wiper blades.

He leans close to whisper, "So you're gonna make a run for it?"

"Maybe."

"How much money you got?"

"Don't know."

"Then you're either a retard or you're lying," says Frankie. "So, are you a retard?"

I stay quiet.

"'Cause I ain't going to waste my time helping no retard who's just going to wind up back inside before the sun goes down."

"I'm not a retard."

"So…how much money ya got?"

"Twenty-six dollars and eighty-eight cents."

"And how far are ya gonna get on twenty-six dollars and eighty-eight cents?"

"I don't know."

"I do," says Frankie. "And that's nowheres. Not without a plan."

He takes another look at Billy.

"This funeral," he whispers. "Where's it to?"

"It's a memorial service."

"Memorial service, funeral, what odds? Where's it to? A church?"

"A funeral home."

"What one? Carnell's? Osgoode's?"

"I don't know."

"Billy," Frankie shouts, "who you dropping first—me or the kid?"

"Sykes," Billy calls back.

"Osgoode's then," says Frankie. "In the east end, just off the highway. So listen. There's a bathroom in the lobby—not the Men's, but the family one—the one with the baby on the picture. You know what I mean?"

I nod.

"Go in there—there's a window what's easy to open. Okay?"

"How do you know?"

"Never mind how I knows," he says. "I just knows. So listen. The window, it's right by the toilet, so you can stand on the seat and reach it. Pop it open—it's on a hinge, so it's not gonna fall out—and crawl on out. Once you're out, just hang down—there's an oil pipe sitting right there, right under the window. Just step on that, then jump. Got it?"

"An oil pipe," I say.

"Right," says Frankie. "Once you're down, there's a fence right in front of you. Head to that and follow it downhill, for—I don't know—ten meters. You come to a hole in the fence, cut right through it. Squeeze on through that…"

"What if I get stuck?"

"Jesus, Cowboy—if I can get through it, you can. So you're through the fence, then you'll see the highway in front of you. Head for that. There's a little path there—a rabbit run, pretty much, but enough to see—and it'll take you to a little brook and a culvert that goes under the highway. Go through that and just there, on the right, there's a concrete pipe—a storm sewer or something. Get yourself into that and wait."

"Wait?"

"For me," says Frankie.

"What about the police?"

"Don't worry about the police—they don't get their arses outta their cars for a murder. For a missing Hollow kid, they might bother to roll down a window, but there's no way they're going to be slogging through no muddy ditch."

"But Mr. Fitzpatrick—Dez—he'll be there."

"Old Dezzy?" says Frankie. "Yeah—he'll be there in his shined-up loafers and his suit and tie. He'll stay farther from the mud than the cops."

Frankie looks out the window.

"We're just coming up to Osgoode's now," he says. "You got all this?"

I nod. "The toilet—"

"The family one."

"The family one. Out the window, through the fence to the culvert, to the pipe, and wait for you."

"Right on," he says. "Now remember—you stay put till I gets there. I'll call out the signal to lets ya know it's me."

"The signal?"

"Three barks, right together," says Frankie, then leans in close to make the noise in my ear. "Ruf, ruf, ruf."

I smile, which is the wrong thing to do.

"Don't be no smart ass," Frankie says. "It's a good signal—been using it for years and the cops still don't know it. Stunned arseholes."

"Okay. Three barks."

Frankie gives me a wink.

"Jesus, Cowboy," he says. "Doing a runner, knowing the signal."

He looks out at the rain, still doing that snail dance to the back of the bus.

"You're one of us, b'y."

Soon as I step into the funeral home I see the family bathroom. Should I go in now or wait till after the service? Before I can decide, Dezzy spots me and calls me over.

"Charlie," he says. "How are you?"

"Okay."

"I guess Mr. Delaney told you what's happening today."

"He told me my dad got cremated."

"That's right. Yesterday."

"So I guess there'll be ashes and stuff."

"There will be, in an urn. You'll see it when we go inside. Child Services will store it for you in a safe place—and you can have it when you turn eighteen. They'll hold his remains for you. They're yours."

Which is a funny thing to say about ashes—'cause how can ashes be anybody's? They're nothing, or as close to nothing as you can make something. They all look the same. I mean, if you really burn something up—all the way, so there's no hair or bone or bark or anything left—every kind of ash looks the same. Which makes me feel sorta good, because what's left of my dad in that urn isn't my dad, is it? The only thing left of my dad is what's in my head. That hockey game we watched, or the time he yelled at me for stealing a sip of his beer. And that stuff will be in me forever, or until I die. "Charlie—any thoughts on that?" says Dezzy.

"Sorry?" I say, not listening again.

"On where you might like to scatter the ashes."

I shake my head. And that's when I decide: I'll go now. I was going to wait till after the service, but now that I think about my dad and the ashes, I don't care if I go to the service, because my dad isn't going to be there anyways.

So I say to Dezzy, "There's one thing I gotta do. I gotta put on a T-shirt—a special one my dad gave me. It's in my backpack."

"Sure. Put it on."

"I gotta pee too. Maybe can I just use the bathroom?"

"Sure."

We're crossing the lobby when I hear a voice call, deep and raspy like it's coming from the bottom of an old bucket full of gravel.

"Charlie, b'y," it calls out. "Jesus, I knowed it was you, soon as I seen ya."

I turn and there's two people coming at me together: Constable Tubby, his belly busting outta his shirt, and this other guy I never saw before. Even so, I know right away who he is. He's got the same curls, same face, same big steps when he walks—same as my dad, except harder, tougher. The hair's grayer and the face has got wrinkles, like how my dad might look if he camped out in the woods for a month.

It's my uncle. Nick Sykes.

Then he's in front of me, kneeling down so he can look me in the eye, stinking of cigarettes when he opens his mouth to talk.

"Jesus, you look like your dad," he says. He's close now, close enough to see he's not exactly like my dad. He's missing two bottom teeth, for one thing. And he's got big old hairs shooting outta his eyebrows and ears, like weeds coming up through a schoolyard in summer.

"That's close enough," says Tubby.

Nick Sykes gives him a glare. "Close enough, my arse," he says. "I'm not on friggin' parole, ya know. This is my nephew, who I never had the chance to meet till today. If I commits a crime with him, arrest me. If not, piss off."

He looks at me again.

"Now," he says, "let your uncle get a good look at ya."

It's when he puts his arms out that I see the hand—the right one, the one sitting on my shoulder. It's a giant claw— the middle three fingers missing, the other two bent inward, black and cracked and wrinkled.

"Looking at my clinker, are ya?" says Nick. He pulls it off my shoulder and holds it up.

"Got that in a fire," he says, then looks up at the cop. "Trying to put it out. Anyways," he goes on, "don't let that bother ya none. It don't hurt no more, and it's got its uses."

He opens it and closes it two or three times, the black nails clicking each time it shuts. He stands up and gives my hair a toss with his good hand.

"You and me should have a talk sometime—after all this racket dies down."

I don't say anything.

"Ya needs ta get ta know yer family, now yer old man's gone. Ya gotta have somebody lookin' out for ya in this world, Charlie, b'y. That's the key to gettin' along."

The hand is back on my shoulder.

"That's the key," he says, looking right at me, the claw giving a squeeze that keeps getting tighter.

Does he know what my dad gave me, back in the hospital? I wonder, trying to pull away from a squeeze that's starting to hurt.

"Family's the key to a happy life," he says, finally letting go. "I mean, if yer family don't look out for ya, who will?"

"We will," says Dezzy, doing his best to look official. "I appreciate you're breaking no laws, Mr. Sykes, but for now, Child Services is Charlie's legal guardian, and it's our job to oversee who he associates with. You're welcome to attend the service, of course,"

"Oh, I appreciates that," says Nick. A bit of spit comes outta his mouth when he says it.

"Sarcasm aside," Dezzy says, "it's a family service so you're free to attend. But I'll be sitting with Charlie, and right now he wants to change into a clean shirt. Charlie?"

We head over the bathroom, and I slip past Dezzy while he holds the door.

"Don't bother locking it," he says. "I'll stand guard out here."

Inside, it's like Frankie said, and soon as Dezzy shuts the door I get up on the toilet seat and open the window.

"All right in there?" Dezzy calls.

"Yup," I say. My heart's beating so fast I figure I could see it thumping in my chest if I looked down. "I'm just having a pee," I say, figuring that'll keep Dezzy on the other side of the door for a bit. But only for a bit, I know, so quick as I can I toss my backpack out the window and go through right behind it, tapping my foot down to find the oil pipe. I'm on it, then on the ground and at the fence. Then down to the right and through the hole in the fence. Except the backpack gets stuck—a wire goes right through it. I pull and pull and finally yank it free. Then take off for the highway without looking back. I don't slow down till I see that culvert, running under the highway just ahead.

It's one of those big old steel culverts, and when I step inside it's all echoey, cars zooming along up above, truck tires *puck-puck*ing across the seams. For a sec, standing there, I feel invisible, thinking how none of those drivers have any idea there's a kid right under them, thinking how all those people back at the funeral home are figuring out—right now— that I took off, and none of them knows, just for this little bit, where I am. No one has got any idea that I'm right here, leaning my backpack against the culvert, thinking the steel looks like ribs inside some giant dinosaur that I'm right in the middle of. Invisible. Except I know I'm not invisible. I know I got to find that storm sewer and climb inside, because sooner or later someone's going to think to have a look under here. So I start through the culvert to the other side.

It's spooky in the middle. Light at both ends, but dark here, the rocks *ponk*ing when I step on them. Just when it gets scariest, when I get a feeling on my neck that makes me shiver my shoulders, it starts to get lighter from the daylight at the other end. Then I'm through and the storm sewer is right there—a round, concrete tube just big enough for me to crawl inside. It's tight. I have to take my backpack off and push it in front of me. But I can keep my feet dry by walking like a crab, shuffling up the side of the pipe. I don't want to get a soaker, with the key being inside my sneaker and all. Every once in a while I look back down the pipe, and when the light at the opening is pretty much just a little dot I stop and wait.

When you wait someplace where there's nothing to do, you start to think about stuff. That's probably why they have those ratty old magazines in the doctor's office—to give you something to think about besides how much your ear hurts. But there's no magazines here, so I start to notice other stuff, like how quick it gets cold in a place where there's no sun—cold that goes right into the middle of you. And about Nick's hand—about if it gets itchy. That's the kind of thing you think about when you're waiting in a dark place where you can't read. If I can't read anything, I can still hear plenty, and what I hear is a *skitter-skitter* behind me, getting closer. Whatever it is sounds big, but everything seems big when you can't see it—like a bump on your leg you find in bed at night and it feels like it must be bigger than a big brown egg, which means it's gotta be cancer, except in the morning you look at it and it's a little pimple. That's how it is with stuff you can't see—it always sounds bigger than it is. Except I suppose it doesn't always. I suppose sometimes it probably is as big and scary as you think, but I guess you don't hear about those times because the person ends up getting eaten by a grizzly bear he thought was a raccoon.

But this isn't a raccoon—I know that for sure because they don't have raccoons in Newfoundland. I read that before we came out here. It could be a rat, though, or a bunch of them. Which I've never seen before because we don't have rats in Alberta. That's true. Not one rat. We've got a Rat Patrol that goes around killing them, right at the border, if any try to sneak in. I'd sure like to see that Rat Patrol right now with their big flashlight and a .22, shining down here to scare off those rats. I think that's what it's got to be. Yes! I see one now, something furry, moving back and forth along the concrete. And another one behind it—and another one. Jesus. I've got to move toward the light, even if it means somebody might see. There's no way I'm going to let a bunch of sewer rats crawl on me.

I scrunch along till I'm right at the opening. And that's when I hear the signal: three barks. I listen for a bit and then it comes again: three more, right together. I stick my foot outta the pipe, then my head, then the rest of me, standing there for everybody to see, blinking in the sun. Except there's nobody to see me; leastways, nobody I can see. But there is a smell—that first draw on a smoke. Then the smoke, too, a puff of it from the other side of the storm sewer, where I can't see. Frankie lighting up, I figure. Until I spot the hand holding the cigarette, right in the middle of those two claws.

"Jesus Christ—still using the old signal," Nick says, stepping out from behind the sewer pipe. He's smiling. "Figured you might—worked good enough for me and yer old man."

I back away, though there's nowheres much to go, the brook behind me, a steep bank in front.

Nick holds up the claw.

"Now don't be running off, Charlie, b'y. I just wants to have a chat, that's all. A bit of a chat. Get to know ya—which ya don't seem so keen on, seein' how's ya took off two minutes after layin' eyes on me."

He puts his black fingers to his lips and sucks in another drag.

"I planned that before I ever knew you were going to be there," I say.

"Figured that," says Nick. "The way ya got outta there— real sharp, like. Figured you musta had a plan when ya come in."

"But how'd you know I'd be here?"

"Didn't," says Nick. "Soon as Mr. Suit and Tie started his hollerin' 'bout you doing a runner, I slipped out and had a boo at the window you got out through. Then I just went where I woulda gone. Found this"—he pulls a bit of blue canvas outta his pocket—"where ya squeezed through the fence. Followed the path. Come to the culvert. Had a look around. Then I seen the storm drain. Listened here for a bit, too, but you was good and quiet. That's when I remembered the old signal."

"I got friends coming," I say. "To pick me up."

"Figured that too. Figured a Fort Mac boy like yerself would need a townie to tell ya where you're to."

"That's right," I say. "My friend—from The Hollow— he told me about the window back there, and the sewer pipe and stuff. And he's coming to get me. Anytime now."

"S'pect he is," says Nick. "S'pect he is. Which is fine by me. I ain't up to no mischief. Jesus, I'm just after gettin' out from inside; I ain't plannin' on puttin' meself back there. No, no, Charlie—I just wants a little chat."

"About what?"

"You, I 'spose. I ain't heard much about you since Mikey went upalong."

"Upalong?"

"Upalong, sure—the mainland," says Nick. "I forgets, yer a Westerner. You looks so much like yer old man, an' not that much younger than the last time I seen him."

He flicks his cigarette into the stream.

"Come 'ere," he says with a nod. "Let me get a better look at ya. Come on, now. I ain't gonna bite."

I step closer, and he puts a hand on each shoulder, then slips his hands under my arms and gives the side of my chest a couple of thumps.

"Yer a strapping lad," he says. Then he squeezes me all of a sudden and picks me up and gives me a shake. I can feel his burned fingers under my ribs, moving, searching.

"And solid all around too," he says, putting me down. Up close I see a scar I didn't notice before, long and thin and white, from the corner of his lip all the way up to the soft bit just under his left eye. He sees my eyes follow it.

"Come precious close to having a patch to go with this hand a mine. A real pirate I'd a been then. Ah, Charlie, but I had a hard old life of it, by times, though there's little of it you knows about."

He leans back and takes a look at me.

"Did ya even know you had an uncle, Charlie, b'y?"

I shake my head.

"Jesus. Yer old man, he didn't say nothin' 'bout me?"

"No."

"Nor why he were comin' out here, on this trip you was on?"

I shake my head again.

"Well," says Nick, pulling a pack of cigarettes from his jacket pocket with those two fingers, "it's a sad thing when a family forgets one another like that."

He digs a smoke out, his fingers clicking like robot hands.

"I means it, Charlie. I means it—it's a terrible thing to be forgettin' yer family. I hope ya got something from yer old man to remember him by—a little keepsake—a letter, a picture. Could be anything—just something to remember him by."

The quiet drags on till Nick speaks again.

"Well, Charlie. Do ya got something?"

"A watch. I got his watch."

"Nothing else?" Nick asks. He's leaning toward me, the scar doing a little zigzag on his face when he squints from the cigarette smoke. "He didn't leave ya nothin' like an old coin? We used to have our own money here, Newfoundland did. He mighta left ya an old Newfoundland nickel. Or a key?"

He wants to sound all casual when he says it, but his eyes never leave mine. They're pinned to me, drilling through the smoke that slips between his lips.

Before I can answer there's the *ponk-ponk* of stones falling down the steep bank. It's Frankie and another kid—somebody I've never seen.

"Cowboy, me old trout," Frankie says when he gets down to the stream. "What are ya at?"

He stops when he sees Nick behind the sewer pipe. "Who's the old guy?"

"Never mind who the old guy is," says Nick. "Who the hell are ye?"

"Old guy's got some mouth on him," says Frankie. "And he's got some hand too. Jesus, Cowboy, where'd buddy come from anyways? The circus?"

Frankie's friend is beside him now. He's taller than Frankie, and wider too. He gives Nick a long look and shoots out a spit while he does it. It hits a big gray rock halfway to Nick and runs down the side.

Nick flicks the smoke away. He glares at Frankie.

"I beat a man till he bled for saying less than that," Nick says.

Frankie's friend gives a laugh, but not Frankie. He shuts right up and looks hard at Nick. Then he nods, the tiniest bit, a nod you wouldn't see if you weren't looking right at him.

"You're Nick Sykes," Frankie says.

"So how come the kid doesn't have the lobster claw?" says the friend. "Or maybe it doesn't run in the family?"

"Shut up, Gerald, b'y," Frankie snaps back at his friend, before turning toward Nick.

"Don't mind him, Mr. Sykes—he's a bit of an arsehole by times."

"I see that," says Nick.

"I didn't know who you was a minute ago there. I'm Frankie Walsh—Roger's boy."

Frankie holds out his hand for Nick to shake, but Nick just lets it sit.

"My old man used to move some stuff through your old man," says Frankie.

"I knows who he is," says Nick. "How's he doing? Still drinkin'?"

"Like a dog at a toilet," says Frankie.

"You best watch yourself around the booze," says Nick. "Ruined yer old man. He coulda done something with himself, 'cept he were pissed all the time."

Nick looks at the friend.

"And who's this turd ya got hangin' from yer shorts?"

The guy looks like he's going to say something, but Frankie shakes his head.

"Gerald—lives up off Logy Bay Road."

"Yacht club kid," says Nick. "Thought his clothes were a bit too pretty for a Rabbit Town punk."

"He's a friend—we hang out," says Frankie.

"Well," says Nick, "I think I'll go search out a friend or two and hang out a bit myself."

He turns to me.

"We'll have ta finish our chat later, Charlie. See if we can't find something for ya to remember yer old man by— like a key what he might a had on him when he died. See if we can't track that down. It'd be a nice thing to have," he says, then starts walking off down the brook.

"A nice thing to have," he says again to himself, but loud enough for me to hear.

FOURTEEN

Gerald's got a car waiting for us on a little street up over the riverbank. It's big and blue, and right away I know it's the nicest car I've ever been in. The inside is black and leather and hot from the sun that came out a while ago, and sitting in it is like being inside a nice, old catcher's mitt.

My dad bought me one of those last year when I signed up for Little League. At first he didn't want me to join, but I kept bugging him because I didn't ever have anything to do all summer except watch TV and go to the store, since Robert always went to his cottage when school got out.

"Like my car, kid?" Gerald says when he sees me looking around.

I nod.

"Ain't his," says Frankie. "It's his old man's."

"But I get to drive it whenever I want," says Gerald.

"So get driving," says Frankie. "To the Cape."

We take off so fast I get thrown back into the seat, then against the window when Gerald swings the car sharp up onto the ramp to the highway. We're only on that for a second when there's another ramp and we're onto a smaller road, two lanes, with lots of hills.

"Gun 'er, b'y," says Frankie. "All the cops is off to Osgoode's, looking for Cowboy."

The car makes a rumble I can feel through the seat and starts going fast, really fast—fast enough that I can't make out anything if I look straight through the side window. Frankie bends down in the front seat, then passes something back to me—a can with beer foaming up through the top. He passes one to Gerald, too, then flips a switch to open up the sunroof. The wind coming in makes a giant roar. Then Frankie presses something on the dash and *boom*, *boom*, *boom* starts shaking the seat. Frankie leans over to yell something in Gerald's ear, and they both have a big laugh. But I can't hear anything except the wind and the music, meaning I can't ask Gerald to watch out for moose, which is what I want to do since this is my first time in a car since the accident.

The music's so loud and the car's going so fast that the beer is foaming outta the can. I'll have to lick some off. And it tastes gross, which I knew it would. It's that way with a lot of stuff grown-ups like. It looks like it should taste good, but you take a sip and it's all bitter and makes your mouth scrinch up so much that you think it might be poison. Anyways, I can't drink this, so I tap Frankie on the shoulder and pass it up to him. He finishes it in one long gulp just when Gerald drives into a big empty parking lot, with a sign that says *Cape Spear, Most Easterly Point in North America.*

And all of a sudden it's quiet. The car is off, the radio's off, the wind is gone and everything's still. Right in the middle of which, Frankie lets out a giant burp that seems to go on for an hour. Then he's outta the car with Gerald right behind him, headed up a wooden boardwalk to a lighthouse up on a cliff.

"Cowboy, c'mon—let's go," Frankie yells down to me. "An' grab that six-pack from the front seat."

A minute later I'm beside them, walking up wooden steps past the lighthouse painted red and white. We go by it and head out farther along the cliff on a path. Off to the right it's miles and miles of scrubby trees and grass and rocks, and on the left there's a couple a feet of grass and the edge of the cliff and then nothing except the ocean way down at the bottom. After a minute or two, Gerald and Frankie go right out to that edge and take a seat, hanging their legs out into the nothing.

"Pass us the beer," Frankie says back to where I'm standing a bit away from the edge. He opens two, passes one to Gerald, then lights a cigarette.

It's quiet now except for the wind and the crash of the waves whapping into the rocks a hundred feet down. Looking out at the ocean, all blue and black and white in the wind, it's like being at the front of a ship, the wind coming in, our jackets snapping in it. Frankie holds out his hand and points with a beer can.

"Whales," he says. I don't see anything at first. Then I spot one, two, three bunches of white spray shooting up into the sky. Then a black tail that flips up and sinks under the water.

"You'll smell 'em in a minute," says Frankie, watching the spray going up. And in a bit I get a whiff of salt and fish mixed together, coming off the water in the wind. Then it's gone, and there's just the wind and Frankie smoking and the beer cans *plonk*ing on the rocks when Frankie and Gerald set them down.

"A rare day," says Frankie, his jacket flying back toward me in the wind like a flag on a pole. "A rare friggin' day."

FIFTEEN

The sun's a big orange half-eaten by the sea when we start back to town. Frankie opens another beer as we drive, and it's quiet with the sunroof closed and the music off. Frankie's quiet, too, just drinking every once in a while and looking out at the trees zipping past. Mostly it's just trees, though once in a while there's ocean and cliffs that run up into St. John's. If I wasn't in a car—if I was walking along, maybe off into the trees a little ways—it'd be like I was in one of those old movies with knights and dragons. That's how it looks with the sun starting to go down, all green hills and gray cliffs that end sharp at the ocean. Just like the edge of a table, with the sea way down below—so far down that when we were out at Cape Spear, seagulls were flying *underneath* our feet.

It's beautiful.

I wouldn't use that word if it wasn't, because it's not a word I use very often—maybe even ever, when I think about it. But it is.

Beautiful.

Then we're in town, just like that. We come over a hilltop and take a windy road down, and there's traffic lights with taxis and dump trucks and corner stores. Farther along toward downtown there's a big hockey rink, all new and concrete. Then there's old wooden houses, squinched all together in rows, each one painted a different color. There's red ones and orange ones and blue ones and even a purple one. I never saw a house painted purple before. Most of the houses back home are white or gray or brown or brick. I never even knew they made purple paint for houses. I thought they only made it for inside rooms and that only girls liked it.

"You hungry?" Frankie says, talking for the first time in about half an hour.

"A little," I say.

"Gerald, drop up to Leo's and we'll grab three mediums and some Pepsis."

Gerald swings the car up a steep hill, past an old church with a spiky fence that's half falling down. When we come over the top of the hill, I see a lot of stuff is half falling down in this part of town. The houses are still in rows, but they're tiny—so tiny I can't believe anybody really lives in them. And they're not reds and blues like the ones down the hill. They're green, like in a hospital, or brown or dirty old white. A lot have paint peeling off or whole bunches of their siding missing.

"The old man's place is just down there," says Frankie, nodding toward a little dead-end street. There's a streetlight at the far end, flickering on and off, with kids standing around underneath. They're chucking a pair of tied-together sneakers at the power lines going to the light. Then the street's behind us and Gerald pulls up in front of a little restaurant, all bright inside.

"Stay where you're to," Frankie says when he gets out. "Even the RNC's smart enough to figure a kid on the run might be wanting to get himself something to eat around suppertime. I'll bring your order out. You want gravy?"

"For what?" I say.

"For your fee and chee, b'y," says Frankie, pointing to the Leo's Fish and Chips sign. "What do you think?"

"But you said gravy."

Frankie nods. "Gravy. For your chips. You want some or not?"

"What kind of gravy?"

"What kind?" says Frankie. He's looking at Gerald, and I can see him push his eyebrows up.

"Jesus Christ, Cowboy. It's brown. That's what kind it is. Brown."

"I never heard of getting gravy from fish," I say, which is my way of being polite, because I *know* you don't get gravy from fish. At least in Alberta you don't. I've had lots of fish— fish fingers, fish fillets, fish nuggets, even a whole big Char from up north. I never got gravy with it. Not once.

"I don't know where they gets it from," says Frankie. "I just know it's brown, and it's good. Now do you want some or not?"

"No," I say.

Frankie and Gerald head to the diner.

"What kind of gravy is it?" I hear Gerald say in a girly voice.

"Stunned mainlander," Frankie says.

Ten minutes later Frankie hands me something wrapped up in plain paper.

"Get that down ya," he says.

"And don't make a mess," says Gerald. "Get any fish on the seat and I'll break yer neck."

I don't get anything on the seat. I eat it all, every last bit. It's the best fish I ever had. The best fish. The best fries. It likely woulda been the best gravy, too, even if it didn't come from a fish. Even with it being so good, I almost can't finish it, till I let out a big Pepsi burp and I'm hungry again.

"Good one, Cowboy," says Frankie, squishing his paper up into a ball. He passes it to Gerald, who reaches back for mine and then chucks it all toward a trash can by the curb. The balled-up papers bounce off the steel mesh and onto the side-walk. But he doesn't get out to pick it up—just starts the car and drives away, which is no better than just chucking the whole mess out onto the sidewalk. I look back, and it's already blowing down the street, the wads coming apart, spreading garbage everywhere. There's lot of garbage around—plastic bags up in trees, pop cans blown against curbs, garbage bags with crows hopping around them. Now our crap is there too. It'll blow around till it bangs into something—a fence, a house, a gate—then it'll get wet and rotten and gross and it'll sit there till somebody scoops it up, or until it gets walked on and walked on till it turns into part of the mud. It makes me kind of sad—all the garbage floating round 'cause everybody's too lazy to do something about it. Me included, I guess.

"We're off to a little party now, Cowboy," Frankie says, turning back to me. "Friend of Gerald's—been away for a bit, and she's having a welcome-home thing. We gotta make one stop on the way to pick up some shit from a guy I knows. Then we'll make like babies and head out. Couple a friends—couple a drinks. You up for that?"

"Guess so."

. It's dark now. The streetlights are on—except for the one on Frankie's street, which is out I see when we drive past, those sneakers hanging from the wire. I don't really think I have much choice besides saying okay. If I said, "No, let me out," what would I do? I don't know anybody here except for Frankie, and, I guess, Dezzy. But if I called him I'd be right back in The Hollow. And I have to admit, eating those fish and chips with Frankie and Gerald is way better than sitting in The Hollow cafeteria, wondering when Flarehead is going to bash my face in.

"Party's out to the Gut," says Gerald, heading back down the steep hill again.

"Quidi Vidi," says Frankie, opening up another beer. "Just behind Signal Hill."

I'm guessing that's the big hill I see right in front of us. There's a big house at the top of it, lit up by spotlights, like a castle stuck up high on a cliff.

"What's the building?" I say.

"Cabot Tower," says Gerald.

"It's where Columbus landed," says Frankie.

Gerald laughs. "What?" he says, turning to Frankie. "You serious or what, b'y?"

"Well," says Frankie, "Columbus or some other prick who come sailing over here."

"Jesus—what do they teach you in that school?" asks Gerald. He looks at me in the rearview mirror.

"Frankie's full of shit," he says. "It's called that after John Cabot—the guy who discovered Newfoundland. The hill it's on is Signal Hill, 'cause they used to run flags up a pole to signal ships coming into the harbor."

"Now who's full of shit," says Frankie. "It's Signal Hill 'cause some wop sent some message off to Italy or somewheres from up there, back before they had phones or anything."

"To Ireland," says Gerald. "A radio signal they sent to Ireland from up there. But that's not why they call it Signal Hill."

"Oh, really," says Frankie, taking another drink. "And I suppose you'd know all about it, Professor."

"Mor'n you," says Gerald. "I'm doing advanced history."

"Oh, Jesus," says Frankie. "You hear that, Cowboy? Advanced history, instead of the stunned-arse history what you and me takes."

He tips the beer so steep it's like he's going to eat the can, then tosses the empty out the window.

"Well, Mister Advanced History," says Frankie, barking a giant burp between *Advanced* and *History*, "if you're such a smart guy, how come you're such a shitty driver?"

Then all of a sudden Frankie grabs the steering wheel and yanks it hard over to his side of the car. Gerald hits the brakes, and the car spins right around, my end swinging in a big circle until—*pow!*—the wheels slam into the curb and we're stopped, pointing the way we were just coming.

"Jesus Christ, Frankie," says Gerald. "What the hell's the matter with you? You coulda killed us."

"You're the matter with me, ya snotty arsehole," says Frankie. Then before Gerald can say anything to that, Frankie hauls back his fist and takes a swing at him. But instead of hitting Gerald, he bashes his hand into the rearview mirror.

"Jesus," Frankie says, grabbing his hurt hand with the other, which gives Gerald the chance to reach past him and open the passenger door. Frankie's bending over, some drool hanging from his mouth while he rubs his knuckles. It's the same hand he busted up on Flarehead, I can see, 'cause it's bleeding again.

"Get the hell out," says Gerald, giving him a shove through the door. He gives another push, and Frankie ends up on the sidewalk.

"And don't be calling me until you sober up, ya dirty pisspot. You're worse'n your old man."

This last bit he says when he's pulling the door shut. I wonder if maybe I should get out with Frankie, seeing as I just met Gerald a little bit ago. But before I get a chance to say anything, Gerald does a U-turn and we're off headed for the party again. He puts the mirror back in place and sees me looking at him.

"Got something to say?" he asks.

Maybe I do, I think. Maybe I got to say that he should let me out so I can check to make sure Frankie's okay. That'd probably be the right thing to say, seeing how Frankie's helped me out twice already. But what could I do? I don't have any bandages or anything. And it's not like I could take him to my house and get him cleaned up and call his mom or dad to come get him. And it might be worse for him with me there anyways, 'cause I can just see a cop car go driving by and then pulling over. I get arrested and they take me into some cement room down in a basement somewheres and keep me up all night, making me sit in a hard chair with some light in my face. And I don't get any breakfast or any lunch or supper and finally I tell them how Frankie helped me break outta the funeral home, and Frankie ends up back in jail, except this time it's a real jail, 'cause he's eighteen, and who knows what could happen to him in a place like that? So it's probably better if I just don't say anything. Which I do, even though when we're driving away I get a picture in my head of that garbage we left on the sidewalk back at the fish and chip place.

"Well?" Gerald asks again.

"Is Frankie drunk?" I know he is, because I've seen my dad drunk. Most times my dad ends up sad, which is how Frankie looked when we were driving off. Once, with my dad, he started off happy when he got home, talking about how he got a raise and that meant more money, and that meant we could move outta the cat-pee place. Then all of a sudden he got all sad about how he made me live in a place that smelled like cat pee. And how he should do better for me, which—honest—was something I never even thought of thinking. Anyways, it all ended up with him crying and me going over to give him a pat on the shoulder, which he didn't much like me to do.

"Leave me alone," he'd say, every time. "Just leave me alone."

So I already know Frankie is drunk, but I ask anyways.

"Yes, Jesus, he's drunk," says Gerald. "First thing he does, every time he gets out—gets pissed. Always starts off good—couple a beer, a drive somewhere. Maybe a draw if he scores something. Then he pulls some crap like this. Every time."

"Sorry," I say. I don't really know why I say it.

"Sorry?" says Gerald. "What do you got to be sorry about?"

"Well," I say, "I guess if you guys hadn't a come to get me, this wouldn't have happened."

"If we hadn't come to get you, some other kind of shit would have happened. Frankie woulda got pissed at something. Guaranteed. Something I said, something somebody else said, a car that cut us off, an old guy looking at us wrong—it'd be something. Guaranteed."

He rolls down the electric window and shoots out a great big spit.

"Anyways," he says, "he'll be okay tomorrow, when he sobers up. For now, I wanna go see this girl who's having this little party. You can come—just don't cause any shit."

"Okay."

We turn off the main street onto a curvy little road where all the houses are jumbled up next to one another. Some are big, some are little, some squished together, other ones sitting off by themselves, up on little hills, with paths running between them. We take a right turn and there's the ocean again—at least I think it's the ocean. It looks the same, gray and cold, but it's almost like a little lake, the banks close to one another.

"Is that the ocean?" I say.

"Quidi Vidi Gut. Ocean comes into the gut through that break in the rocks."

He stops the car and lowers my window. The moon's starting to come up now, and right below it there's an opening in the rocks, with big waves rolling in. It's cold outside, and wet, too, with a mist that floats into the car.

"Fog coming in," says Gerald. "We won't be sitting out tonight."

A couple a secs later we pull into a driveway, right up beside a house. It's a big one, painted red and yellow to make it look old-timey, but you can tell it's new. It's full of windows, one beside the other, going from the floor to the ceiling, like whoever built it wanted to make sure everybody could look in and see all the stuff they owned. "Take your backpack," Gerald says when I get out of the car. "I don't know how long I'm staying, and I don't want your crap in the car when I take off."

Gerald goes up the steps and rings the bell while I wait at the bottom. Someone answers: a girl.

"Where've you been?" she asks. "You get the stuff?"

"Jesus," says Gerald. "Nice to see you too."

"Sorry. It's just I've been waiting."

"The wait's gonna be a little longer," says Gerald. "My guy...we had, ah, a little disagreement on the way over here— before we scored the shit."

"Jesus, Gerald."

"Don't worry—he'll be around tomorrow. We can set something up for then. Anyways, I got some beer for tonight..."

He holds up another six-pack.

"'Kay," says the girl. "C'mon in."

"And I got a guy with me," he says, waving me up the steps.

I come up and the door opens wide, and it's Clare, standing right there. As soon as she sees me, her eyes get big and she puts her hand up to her mouth.

"Charlie," she says. "Jesus, get in here."

She shuts the door quick behind us.

"You know one another?" Gerald asks.

"We met," says Clare, "when I was in rehab and Charlie was in The Hollow." She turns to Gerald. "And you two have been driving around all afternoon?"

"Had a spin out to the Cape, then something to eat up to Leo's."

"Jesus, Gerald. The whole freakin' city's out looking for Charlie. It's all over the TV—I was just watching it. Anybody see you come here?"

"Don't think so."

"Well, bring your stuff in here, Charlie, and stay right there," she says. "Gerald, help me get these blinds down. Jesus."

"Relax, girl. It's not like he's a murderer or something."

"He's not, but his uncle is. Nick Sykes."

She pulls the last blind down.

"Oh Jesus, Gerald—he's not your connection, is he? You weren't buying off Nick Sykes?"

"No, no," says Gerald. "I mean, I don't know who we were buying off—my buddy, Frankie, he was getting the stuff. I was just giving him the money and driving him to the guy's house to make the pickup. I don't figure this Nick Sykes has even got a house, the way he looked today."

"You saw him?"

"Yeah. Right when we got Charlie, out by the funeral home."

"You helped Charlie get away?" says Clare, like she can't believe it.

"Yeah. Me and Frankie."

"And who's Frankie?" Clare asks.

"Guy I got to know last year. Sold me some dope, started hanging out a bit. You never met him."

"And this Frankie," she says slow, "he got you involved in this whole thing with Charlie." Clare turns to me. "This is Frankie from The Hollow? The older guy you were hanging with at the fence—the guy smoking, with the black hair and the T-shirt?"

I nod.

"And he's the guy who's supposed to be getting my Oxy?"

Gerald nods.

"And he's where now?"

"Last I seen he was sat on his arse on the boulevard."

"And does he know you were coming here?"

"Well," says Gerald, "he knows we were coming to see somebody in the Gut, but he don't know you, and he don't know this house."

"Good," says Clare.

"You're awful snotty about the company you keep, all of a sudden," says Gerald.

"What do you mean?"

"I mean you'd a been happy enough to see Frankie and me if we had a bottle of Oxy with us."

"Not if it meant the cops were two steps behind the pair of you," says Clare. "I mean, Jesus, Gerald. I'm just outta rehab a day. I don't want to get chucked back in again."

"Then maybe you shouldn't be asking me to hook you up with that shit."

"Oh, don't worry. I won't make that mistake again."

Right then I figure Gerald's going to storm out, but he doesn't. Fact, they keep yelling about how Gerald's always getting Clare in trouble and about how Clare always seems happy enough to go along with what Gerald wants to get up to. They keep going on for a long time—long enough for me to take a look round the house. Mostly what I see are books, all about money and banks and economics, that look like they've been opened maybe once. There's some big books about art and museums too. Which makes sense, since they've got a couple a big paintings on the wall. One looks like somebody took a fat paint brush and painted whatever they felt like with a bunch of different colors. They're all squiggled up, angry-like. Another one's got cranberries dumped in a big blue bowl. It's pretty good, how much they look like cranberries. I don't paint, but if I did I wouldn't paint cranberries. I'd paint cop cars, or trains. Still, I bet painting a cranberry is tougher than you might think. It might *seem* easy—what's a cranberry except a red circle? But try sitting down and painting one up that doesn't look like a red circle. I bet that's hard.

There's other things up on the walls too: certificates for certified accounting—stuff like that. And right beside that, a little framed box full of spoons or knives or something. I go up close to take a look and I see they're not spoons—they're keys, brass ones, silver ones, old rusty ones and—yes, right there—one just like the key I got in my sneaker. They're all stuck on green felt, and there's writing underneath: *Honoring a century of shared security between Diebold and The Bank of Nova Scotia, September 27, 2001.*

"You into keys?"

It's Clare, finished her fight with Gerald.

"I never saw keys like this," I say. "What do they open?"

"Locks," Clare says.

"Padlocks?"

Clare leans toward the keys. I smell her hair when she gets close.

"Safety deposit boxes," she says.

"What're those?"

"Boxes," she says. She looks at me like I'm about three years old. "In a bank. You've been in a bank, right?"

"Not in one. I go the teller machine sometimes with my dad, but I never been inside one."

"God, I spent half my life in them, waiting for my old man to finish up work."

"What's he do?"

"He's a manager. Central branch, downtown on Water Street."

"So he's got keys like this to open up these boxes inside."

"Anybody can have a safety deposit box. You just pay your rent each year and the bank gives you a box and a key."

"How big are they? The boxes?"

"Different sizes," says Clare. "Little ones, for things like a will. Bigger ones for jewelry or old books. People put all kinds of things in them."

"And nobody else can get into this box without that key?"

Clare nods. "You show up, tell them your key number, they take you to your box and you open it and get whatever you want out." She gives her head a tilt. "What do you care about that stuff? You're a kid."

"Just wondering. Sometimes when I…"

Right then the doorbell rings, with Gerald coming outta the kitchen to open it.

"Leave it shut," Clare whispers.

Gerald tries to sneak a look out a side window by the door but shrugs his shoulders. "All's I see is a cab," he says. "Can't tell who it is."

The bell rings again, but we all stay where we are.

"Charlie," says Clare. "Quick, go out back to the kitchen. There's a little cupboard by the back door. Get inside and stay quiet."

I start to say something, but she gives me a shove.

"Go," she says. "Leave your backpack and stuff and go."

I'm squeezing into the cupboard when I hear the three barks. Then again, loud and clear, just like this afternoon. Next comes a creak—Gerald opening the front door.

"Frankie," I hear him say. Then back to Clare, "It's just Frankie. Get in here, b'y, you must be freezing your arse off. Sobered up, have ya?"

"Enough to spot yer old man's car," I hear him say. I open the door a crack to get a look, but I can't see anybody.

"Where's Charlie to?" asks Frankie.

"Upstairs," says Clare. "In the bathroom."

"Okay," Frankie says. "You two gotta come out here, just for a sec."

"Screw that," says Gerald. "Get your arse in here."

"Listen," says Frankie, "I got your stuff—my man's here with it. But he don't want to come into no house, so he says for you two to come out and do the deal in the cab. C'mon. He's getting nervous."

"Let me get a coat," says Clare, and a second later the door shuts and I hear them all go down the steps. They're gone maybe a minute, and then they're tramping back up. The front door creaks open again and I hear footsteps, heavy and fast, heading up the stairs to the second floor. I've got my eye to the crack trying to peek out when another eye pops into the opening, about an inch from mine. It's Clare. She pulls the door open and stands there looking pale and like she's gonna scream, except she holds up her finger to her lips. Her whole hand's shaking, and so is what's she's got in it—a pill bottle that's rattling as it jolts up and down.

"He's here," she says in a crazy whisper. "Nick. He found Frankie sitting out on the boulevard. Came out here with him in a cab. He knows you're here, Charlie, but I told him you were upstairs. He's there now, looking, so you gotta go. Now. Straight out back. There's a fence, but there's a hole underneath it—where the neighbor's dog gets in. Go. Now. Go."

She hands me my jacket and gives me a push through the back door. Mist wets my face soon as I step onto the deck—it's thick, swirling around orange in the streetlights. I step toward the fence, and one of those motion-detector spotlights clicks on behind me. Looking back at the house, I see a face looking down at me from a window—Nick, who, soon as he sees me, disappears.

I race for that hole in the fence and squeeze under, the smell of worms and wet in my nose. I'll never fit—it's got to be a small dog—but I got to keep trying 'cause the screen door just slammed shut and there's footsteps flying my way. I pull again and the skin on my back peels down along with my jacket.

It clumps into a ball that holds me until a board breaks and I'm through and running on the other side.

"Charlie," Nick shouts through the fence, but I don't look back. I just keep running up a hill that turns from grass to rocks and roots as I go higher. It looks like I'll be at the top of the hill soon, but all of a sudden I see it's not the top of the hill, it's fog—thick as a cloud, cold and gray and soaking as soon as I step inside it. I run another sec, then stop and turn to look back down at Clare's house, but all I see is a big orange ball where the streetlight is. No house, no fence, no road, nothing except this gray that I feel on my face and my hands, making little drops on my eyelashes and my lips. I take a sec to slow down my breathing, because I know if I can't see Nick, he can't see me.

I wait to hear a scream or a gun or something from down below, but there's nothing until the screen door on Clare's deck gives a screech that ends in a bang. I wait another good while, but it stays quiet. There's not even a car, which means Gerald and Nick and Frankie and Clare are all still down there. Somewhere far off a fog horn starts blowing, and that starts a dog barking—maybe the one who lives next door to Clare.

That bark sounds pretty clear, even though the fog is getting thicker. And now the dog's howling in between barks. Maybe it knows the moon's there, even if it can't see it through the fog.

I start moving up the hill, slow so I'm quiet, but not quiet enough.

"Charlie," Nick calls. He's below me, off toward Clare's house, I guess, but I can't really tell. There's no left or right up here, just a center, where I am, with everything swirling around.

"Charlie," he calls again. "I hear ya out there. It's no good tryin' to get away, ya know. The little girl's neighbor down there, he gave me lend of his beagle. He's a huntin' dog, Charlie, knows these hills better'n the rabbits do. I give him a sniff of your T-shirt, Charlie, b'y—the one you left in your pack, down to the girl's. She's a cute one, Charlie. Maybe you fancies her a bit—I can see why, sure. So come on down to my voice, and we'll hike back to her place. What do ya say, b'y?"

I stay quiet.

"C'mon, Charlie. I don't mean ya no harm. Fact, I'm trying to do ya a good turn here—it's dangerous up on these hills at night, in fog. You're on solid ground one minute and down off a cliff the next. So whaddaya say, Charlie? C'mon back down and we'll have a chat at the little girl's place."

All the while he's saying this, I'm moving slow up the hill, away from his voice. It's getting steeper and I'm on all fours some of the time, feeling the rock in front of me. Parts are too steep to climb, so I have to feel my way around them, till there's a bit I can get up. Whenever I stop, I hear the dog howling behind me. Finally I reach a rock wall, pretty much straight up, as far as I can feel. I go down each way along it a good piece, but there's no way around it—I'll have to go up.

It's easy at first, with those little trees growing outta the cliff—they must be able to grow just about anywheres. But they run out soon enough, and now I've got to reach up, feeling around for a crack to grab while I pull myself up. Twice my feet slip and I think I'm headed for the bottom before they touch on something that holds me. Each time I fall far enough to rip my jeans; the second time I start to bleed— I feel blood, warm on my leg, which is about the only warm thing on me. My feet are freezing and my hands are worse, paining each time I shove them into some handhold. I try to blow some hot air onto them when I get a foothold, but each time I stop, I hear that dog getting closer, till it seems he's right down underneath me, though how far that is, I don't know. It seems I been on this cliff for an hour, but for all I know Nick could just reach up here and grab my foot, or my sneaker—the one with the key inside.

I'm just thinking that when I hear his voice down below, louder than ever.

"Charlie, b'y, you up there?"

I hear him moving around, his jacket scraping against the granite as he feels for a branch to grab.

"Charlie," he calls up. "Stay where you're to. I'll come up and give ya a hand getting down outta here."

There's no way I'm going down. I pull my right hand out of a crack and feel for another one. It's bleeding now too. I pull myself up again, ten centimeters, fifteen. And all of a sudden it's like I just stuck my head out from under the blankets on my bed—the fog's gone, the air is clear, the moon is bright. I look down and it's still gray, but my head's in the clear, sitting on top of the fog bank like the top of a pin poking through a cotton ball. The top of the cliff is just above me, with a tree at the edge, close enough to grab. One more heave and I roll onto solid ground, my chest moving up and down, my legs shaking.

"Sing out, Charlie, so I know where you're to," Nick calls from below.

That's enough to get me up again, and I look for the best place to run. It's empty up here, nothing but rocks and grass and tiny trees. In the moonlight I can see little paths running everywhere, but they don't seem to go anywhere in particular—just off in every direction, wide enough for a rabbit but not much else. There is something, though, off to the left—that Cabot Tower Frankie talked about, dark against the sky. There's streetlights around it, and a parking lot. Maybe people, too, even though I don't see anybody. I might not be able to see anything for long, though, because there's more fog over that way, drifting in from the ocean toward the tower. In another couple a minutes it'll disappear, so I take off running for it.

It's hard to run with all these roots going everywhere. Plus there's boggy mud puddles, and it's not long before my feet are soaked, then my pants, all the way to my knees. I bend down to tie up my sneakers good and tight—some of the mud puddles are deep enough to pull my sneaker right off—and that's when I see Nick standing up at the cliff edge, maybe a hundred meters behind me. I'm crouched down so he doesn't see me yet, but he's looking—turning left and right, trying to spot me.

"Charlie," he calls. "Charlie, b'y. Are ya up here? Charlie?" He turns round to call back over the cliff. "Are ya all right?"

He doesn't know if I made it to the top—he's thinking I might have fallen right past him in the fog, and that I could be laying down below, with my neck broke. If I just stay put, down in these roots…But then there's that barking and howling again, and up comes the neighbor's dog, racing along the cliff edge to Nick. Nick pulls something from his shirt and shoves it in the dog's nose, and the dog starts running, right toward me, with Nick just behind. So I'm up again. Nick's getting closer. He'll be on me before I get to the tower, so I shift to the right and run straight toward the fog bank—maybe I can hide in there somehow. Can I run that far? My legs are paining, my lungs too—like I been punched in my chest.

Then I trip and fall face-first, right into a bog, so now I'm soaked all over, and spitting out bits of twigs and probably rabbit poop and who knows what else is sitting in a pond up on top of Signal Hill. I wipe the goop from my eyes and look back, and it seems like Nick must be right on top of me, with that yowling beagle just in front of him. I can't get up—my legs are like noodles, but the fog's only a few meters away so I get on my knees and then on my feet and let myself fall forward, hoping my feet will move in time to keep me from falling flat again. They do, and a sec later I'm in the fog, thicker than ever, the world gone white. If it weren't for that dog, I could stay put and catch my breath, but I know he'll be right behind me, so I keep moving.

Nick, though, seems to have stopped, because the next time he calls out, his voice is farther away.

"Charlie," I hear. "Stop, b'y—stop where you're to. I means it. Don't move."

Whatever he says after that I don't hear because my next step sends me down into another bog hole. A deep one, I think, waiting for my foot to hit the muck. Except it keeps going, and now the rest of my body is following it down, down, down, not into a muck hole but over a steep bank, a cliff. Then my whole body's over the edge, sliding down, impossible to stop, until…I don't know. I don't know what happened, or what I hit, or where I am. I just know my head hurts, my back hurts, and everywhere else is cold, cold, cold. That's all I know for a minute, that I'm feeling bad and cold. Then I feel sick, like I gotta throw up, and all at once that fish and chips comes roaring back up through my throat and mouth and nose, with me flopping onto my side to keep it off my chest.

I lay there a minute with my eyes closed. I breathe in and out, cool now, but in a good way, like you feel after you throw up, so much better it's almost a good feeling. I open my eyes, expecting to see big pile of puke beside my head, but there's nothing. And I mean nothing—just air. I put my arm out to feel round through the fog and it flops straight down, like it's falling over the edge of a table. I'm just starting to figure out where I am when a gust of wind comes up and the fog lifts off me, my head out from under that blanket again, and I see the world clear in the moonlight.

Straight out from me, where I'm laying on my side, there's only night and stars and the ocean. I roll onto my back, and up above there's a black wall of rock that goes straight up, maybe twenty meters. I'm on a ledge sticking out from the cliff, and if

I'm twenty meters from the top, it's got to be another hundred down to the ocean. I can hear the waves banging into the rocks. I try and sit up to get a better look, and that's when I feel a stab go through my ankle, hurting so bad that I give a little cry out. I'm thinking it must be broken when I hear Nick calling to me.

"Jesus Mother Mary," he says, his head sticking out over the cliff.

"Christ, Charlie. You okay?"

"I think my leg's broke."

"It don't look great, that's sure," says Nick. "Can you move at all?"

"Not my leg. But I can move my hands and stuff."

I show him.

"Well, don't Jesus move anything," he says. "You're on a wee bit of a ledge, and it's a long way down, so ya gotta stay still—right still. Okay?"

"'Kay."

"Now, listen. I gotta go for help."

"Can you hurry? My leg's starting to hurt."

"I'll hurry," he says.

He disappears, then comes back a second later.

"Charlie, b'y," he says. "Listen—I gotta know something. And I means it, now. I wants ya to tell me the truth about that key—will ya do that? It's like, you do me a good turn and tell where that key is to, an' I does ya one and gets the fire boys."

I want to say something to that—about how I figure calling for the fire department when someone could fall off a cliff into the ocean is not really a favor. But it's not much of a time to make an argument like that, stuck up a cliff with a broken leg and your pants and jacket all wet and no way up or down. So I don't say anything except decide that it's okay to lie a bit when somebody's being unfair in an emergency.

So I say, "I don't have it."

"But you knows what I'm talking about."

"I guess so."

"A key. Small, brass. Got a number on it."

"I guess so."

"Well, that's meant for me," says Nick. "Yer old man was bringing that to me. Understand?"

I don't say anything.

"It's not valuable or nothing," he says, "but I needs it. You hear me, Charlie?"

"Yep."

"So, listen. I needs ya to do something. I needs ya to promise me that once I gets you outta this mess, you'll get that key to me, all right? Promise me that, Charlie, b'y. Do you hear?"

"I promise."

"Swear it on your father's soul," says Nick. "C'mon. Swear it."

"I swear."

"On what?"

"On my father's soul."

"Good man. Now you just holds on a bit—I'll have them fire guys up here pronto."

Then he's gone, and it's just me and the wind and a hundred meters of nothing.

SIXTEEN

I don't remember much about the rescue, which is sad, because it's the sorta thing I'd usually run out to see. You know, I hear a siren and I run to see if it's a fire truck, a cop car, an ambulance. Every time, like I can't help it.

"Pavlov's dog," my dad called me after I jumped up one time from supper three times in about a minute. Pavlov was this Russian guy back in the 1890s who figured out dogs start drooling when they think about food—like if you always rang a bell before you fed them, they'd start drooling when they heard the bell even if there wasn't any food there. Anyways, my dad was right to say sirens are like a bell to me. Not everyone's like that. My dad, for instance. He'd hear a siren and he'd just sit there, didn't look out the window, just sit.

"Nothing good ever came to me on the other end of a siren," he said once.

So you can see it's kinda sad that all these sirens and flashing lights and firefighters with rescue gear and ropes and metal baskets and their radios all turned up and squawking— all of it was coming right *to* me, right *at* me—and I don't really remember it.

I do remember watching Nick's head disappear, and looking out at the ocean and seeing stars up there. And some stars were moving in a little group, getting closer, and I wondered if I was dying and this was the light everybody talked about in some tunnel that you're supposed to go through when you die. Except these were tiny lights, and those death lights are supposed to be bright. I figured it was a ship coming into St. John's. Then I looked at the moon for a bit, and I musta fallen asleep, because when I opened my eyes again there was the moon, right in my face. I could see the man in the moon clear as day. Then a hand reached out and I thought that didn't make any sense because the man in the moon doesn't have arms. I heard somebody talking and a radio made a squawk and that woke me a bit, just when the man in the moon was moving my hurt leg back and forth. And I heard a yell, which came from me. And the man in the moon turned into a fireman, who was hanging off some ropes. He was talking, but I don't really know what he said. It was windy and cold and black, then bright and cold and swayey. And there was a siren, but it didn't come close and then go away—it just stayed the same and I was right inside it, going up and down, up and down. Then there were nurses and doctors. And my leg hurt again. And I remember another yell, from me.

I had that same feeling I did right after the accident with my dad, when I woke up and opened my eyes and I saw a place I never saw before. But waking up to someplace you've never seen, ever, is weird. So it was like that again, except I knew right away it was a different hospital, because there was a painting of a rainbow on the wall and clouds and a sun with sunglasses on and a big smile. And it made me feel better, seeing that, which sounds silly, I know, 'cause it's really a thing for little kids, like three-year-olds. Most of the time, if I saw something like that painted on a wall, I'd hardly even notice, and it wouldn't make me smile or anything. But when you wake up and don't know where you are, except it's in a hospital and your leg is smashed up, seeing something like a smiley sun makes you feel better.

There are doctors and nurses coming in and out all the time, and last night the big doctor came and talked to me. You can tell he's the big doctor, because for quite a while before he shows up, nurses are busy doing a bunch of stuff getting ready for him—writing down my temperature and putting papers together on a clipboard and saying, about ten times, "Dr. Misky (or Mingy or something like that) will be here in a little bit to have a chat." And then there's a swirl of wind and he's there. It's like when the principal comes into your class because you've been extrabad and everybody all of a sudden sits up and pays more attention. Dr. Misky's got about ten other doctors behind him. Then he says, with a look down at the cast on my leg, "You won't be needing running shoes for a while."

I think he figures I'm going cry when he says that, because right away he says, "But don't worry—you'll be running before you know it. It's just a severe sprain. The cast will stabilize it."

But that's not why I feel like crying—it's because all of a sudden I remember I haven't seen my sneakers since I came in here, and how long ago was that? How long has it been since I had the key with me? And where is it now?

"Nurse," I say, soon as the big doctor and his herd of little doctors leave. "Do you know where my sneakers are?"

"No."

"Could you find out? If it's not too much trouble?"

"They could be anywhere, my luv. The paramedics might've cut them off, or they might have left them in the rig."

"They're my only sneakers."

"Tell you what. I'll check with Property on my way out. They'll have your jacket and other clothes there, bagged up. All right?"

"Thanks."

"And if they're not there, my luv, what odds? You can always get another pair just the same."

Not exactly, I think, but I don't say anything except "Thanks" again.

<hr />

Next morning Nurse comes in and tells me my sneakers are downstairs in Property.

"Can I get them?" I say.

"What do you want an old pair of sneakers for?" says Nurse. I figure I must look like I'm gonna cry again, because right away she says, "Oh, all right—I suppose they remind you of happier days. Tell you what. On my break we'll walk down together and get them—Doctor wants you up and around on that leg, anyways. Will that do you?"

I nod and Nurse shows up just at 10:00 AM, carrying a pair of crutches.

"Here, Charlie—try these. We'll get 'em set for your height."

When I was a little kid, I thought it would be cool to have a cast and crutches. People'd line up to sign it, and they'd want to tap on it and know how it felt to have it on. Except now I got one and I'm trying to walk and all it is is a pain in the butt. And it hurts too.

"You're doing good, Charlie," says Nurse. "We'll just take the elevator to the basement. Property's right beside the pharmacy."

A minute later we're alone on the elevator. I think putting paintings or photographs in elevators would be a good idea, because, as soon as we get in, we both start looking around at stuff—like you do in an elevator. I think that's why they play music in elevators—so you have something to listen to, which takes care of your ears. But there's never anything for your eyes to do except dart around looking at the buttons and the floor and the tiles on the ceiling, and every once in a while, at the person standing across from you, who's doing the same thing.

While I'm thinking about that, Nurse says something I don't hear.

"Sorry?"

"How's your leg doing?" she asks again, looking at my cast, which is the most interesting thing to look at in the elevator.

"Okay."

Finally the doors open into the basement. Everything's pale green down here, even me and Nurse. Our skin looks like we just got pulled out of a lake, after falling in a week before. There's one little pool of bright light, which we walk past. It's a little pharmacy, with some magazines and toothpaste and pill bottles.

"Here we are," says Nurse. She looks into a little room with *Property* written over it. There's a door into it—one of those doors split in two, so the bottom half is closed and the top half open. But the top half isn't really open—it's covered in Plexiglas that's got a hole cut in the middle, with a man standing on the other side. Nurse fills out a slip of paper and slides it to him, and he goes off and comes back with a bag of stuff.

The guy behind the Plexiglas passes the bag to Nurse through a slot and looks down at me while I sign a piece of paper that says I got my stuff back. Just looks and doesn't say a word. It's sort of a waste of a hole—the thing that's cut in the Plexiglas—as far as I can see.

"Well, Charlie," says Nurse, "let's get this gear back up to your room and stowed in the closest. I've got a feeling you'll be getting out soon."

Which means something's up that I don't know about. Anytime a grown-up says something like that—"I've got a feeling" or "I suspect" or "I think maybe this is going to happen"—it means they've already decided it's going to happen. Or their boss has already decided it's going to happen. Like when a teacher says, "I have a feeling the field trip to the park next Wednesday may be cancelled"—well, get ready to be stuck in school next Wednesday.

"What do you mean?" I say.

"Just that you're doing better—your leg looks good. You're just about ready to head home."

I'm just thinking about what to say to that when Nurse's pager goes off. She looks down at it and gives a little quick breath.

"Oh, Charlie, I've got to run. Can you make it back to the room yourself with those crutches? The elevator's right there. Okay, my luv? I'll drop your bag on your bed," she says. Then she's down the hallway and going through the doorway to the stairs, which gives you an idea about how fast the elevators are in here.

With Nurse gone it's suddenly quiet—that extra kind of quiet you feel when a place that's big and busy goes still. Like a hockey rink in the summertime. And that's what it feels like now, knowing there's five floors of beds and doctors and bathrooms and oxygen tanks and stuff sitting right above my head, but down here it's dark and still and quiet. Then there's a guy coming outta the pharmacy just in front of me.

"Charlie," he says. "Thought I might see you when I was in here."

It's Nick, standing there with a pill bottle in his hand.

"Painkillers," he says. "Oxy-something they calls it—for the ankle sprain I got traipsing around Signal Hill the other day. Dangerous spot up there, if you're not careful."

He looks behind him, along the hallway, where there's nobody.

"But I guess you'd know all about that, 'cause it looks like you got hurt."

He nods at my cast.

"I fell."

"Fell, did ya?" says Nick, his voice going up high, making a point that he sounds surprised. "Because I didn't know nothing about that, Charlie. I heard there was some kid hurt up there the other night—that the cops got a...whaddaya call it...an anonymous tip about somebody going over the cliff. But I don't know no details."

He gives me a hard look. "You understand?"

He takes a step toward me, so I back up till I'm right against the wall.

"Now, Charlie," he says, leaning in to me. "Have the cops asked you anything about that? Because no doubt they're wondering how ya come to be up there."

I shake my head.

"Well, they will. And it'd be best if ya didn't really remember too much—ya wouldn't want to get yer man Frankie in trouble, or that pretty thing. Clare, I thinks her name is."

"I wouldn't."

"Course not," says Nick. "Because that Clare's such a pretty thing—and such a sad story too. She's been hooked on these"—he holds up the pill bottle and gives it a shake—"for a couple of years, off and on. Her parents are frantic, putting her into rehab—it almost makes me want to cry, the more she tells me about it."

"She didn't tell me about that stuff," I say.

"Well," says Nick, "she's taken a bit of a liking to me, for some reason"—he drops the pill bottle into his shirt pocket— "telling me all about her life and such. Maybe she's a kindred spirit, do ya think? But she's a fragile thing, Charlie—twice tried to kill herself. Can you imagine? I don't really think anyone'd be too surprised if she managed to do it one of these days, which would be a sin. And ya wouldn't want anything like that on yer head, would ya, Charlie?"

"On my head?"

"Yes, b'y. If ya were to be talkin' to the cops 'bout what happened at the funeral home, and about how you was down to Clare's when she were buyin' drugs, and how you runned away out the back—all that. If you was to tell them about all that, sure they'd be down to her place, sirens screamin' and lights flashin', all the neighbors out on the street, her hauled off in handcuffs, shoved back into that rehab, gettin' it all wrote up in the paper an' on the TV. It'd be enough to drive anyone over the edge, Charlie. And she's right on the edge, b'y. That's my feelin', anyways, from talkin' to her these last few days, since you been shut up in here after yer fall. It was a fall, was it, Charlie? I only knows what I heard on the news. Right?"

I nod.

He looks across the hallway as a couple of people go into the pharmacy.

"C'mon," he says. "I'll go with ya back to yer room—make sure ya makes it okay."

We step into the elevator, which is sitting there, door open. It closes slow, and Nick turns to look at me.

"Gives us time for a bit of a chat, what, Charlie?"

I'd really like a picture to look at now, I think, pressing *Four*. Cranberries'd be nice.

"There is something I do wants to talk to ya about, Charlie, just between me and thee."

We pass One.

"I been thinkin' about what ya said, back the other night. About how ya didn't have the key on ya. Remember that—how ya said you could get it?"

We pass Two.

"An' that got me wonderin' 'bout where that key could be to, Charlie. 'Cause if it weren't on ya, it would have to be with yer stuff, right? Except it weren't. Which I know 'cause I had a little look through yer pack, back to Clare's. An' it weren't there."

We're at Four when Nick moves to the panel and shoves his claw into the Door Closed button.

"Which I figure means ya had it on ya, back at the cliff."

I don't say anything.

"And I thinks to meself, if that was me, where would I put that key?"

He gives a chuckle. "Now, me havin' spent a good few years inside, I knows of a place or two to stow something that you don't know anything about. So ruling out those spots, I think, where would I put that?"

There's a bang on the elevator door, then a voice, dull through the steel. "You all right in there?"

"In my shoe, I thinks," says Nick, looking at me hard.

There's more banging. "You need help in there?"

Nick lets go of the button and the door slides open, with three of four people standing on the other side.

"Friggin' hospital elevators," says Nick, putting his hand out so I can walk in front of him. "Broke down half the time, and slow as cold spit the other half."

He walks beside me as I head for my room, slow on the crutches.

"So where are they, Charlie—those shoes? I see they ain't on yer feet."

We're almost at the room now. I look ahead and see Nurse in there—she must be finished her call—hanging up my shirt in the wardrobe. My jacket's sitting on the bed, and the sneakers are there, right beside it.

I stop before we reach the room, which Nick doesn't know is mine.

"Well," he says, "you got them? Up here in yer room? Or are they downstairs to Property?"

Just then Nurse pipes up, "Charlie, my luv, I'm just after putting your clothes away, so they'll be all ready for you when you leave."

Nick's eyes light up soon as he hears Nurse, and he moves toward the room. But just then the stairway door bursts open beside us, and out tumbles Tubby, all red-faced and bent over.

"Friggin' hospital elevators," he says, staring down at the hallway tiles as he works hard to catch his breath, hands on his knees. He looks up at me, looking at him, and I turn away to see where Nick is.

But he's gone.

SEVENTEEN

While Tubby catches his breath, Dezzy comes round the corner with Miz right behind him—the old gang, all coming to talk to me. Which they do a couple a minutes later when I'm sat up in bed, my clothes and sneakers tucked away in the closet. Looking up at those three staring down at me, I think that somewhere, somebody has definitely decided something.

"Charlie," says Dez, "we've got a bit to talk about this morning. About what's going to happen to you in the next while. But before we get into that, Sergeant Grimes wants to ask a couple of questions. Okay?"

I figure that's one of those questions with just one answer, like, "You do want to pass grade four math, don't you?"

"'Kay."

"Now," says Tubby, getting his notebook out. "First off: Who helped you make your getaway from the funeral home?"

"What you mean 'getaway'?" I ask.

"He means when you left the funeral home without permission," says Dez.

"Didn't know I needed permission. You guys aren't my dad."

"No," says Dez, "but you're smart enough to know you shouldn't leave someplace without telling a grown-up where you're going."

"Well," I say, "I still didn't know I needed to ask anybody's permission."

"Forget this permission crap," Tubby butts in. "Nobody asks permission to escape, and that's what this was—an escape you planned out before. More than that, you had some help, because you can't tell us you just walked into the bathroom and figured you could hop up on the toilet and make a break."

"I didn't plan anything," I say. "I just kinda panicked thinking about those ashes. So I took off."

"Without any help?" says Tubby.

I nod.

"So how'd you end up on Signal Hill?" he says.

"Took a bus."

"Buses don't run out by the funeral home."

"I walked till I found one."

"You mean you walked for miles down the highway looking for a bus, right when half the RNC was out looking for you."

"I never saw any cops."

"Why doesn't that surprise me," says Dezzy.

"So," Tubby goes on, ignoring him, "you got on this mystery bus and it took you where?"

"Downtown."

"Where downtown?"

"Don't know. Just downtown. Near those jellybean houses."

"So you're downtown, by yourself…at what? Three in the afternoon? Four? Suppertime?"

"I don't know."

"So how'd you end up on Signal Hill? Take a bus up there too, did ya?"

"No. I walked."

Tubby gives a snort. "So you're downtown, by yourself, don't know the city, don't know anybody in it, and you decide to walk up to the top of Signal Hill in the dark?"

"Wasn't dark when I started."

"But it was late afternoon—the sun was starting to go down. And you decide to head off to the top of the hill?"

"I saw the tower up there—Cabot Tower."

"And what?" says Tubby. "You thought it was a hotel?"

"I didn't really know what it was. It looked like an old castle—kind of empty up there, all alone. I figured maybe I could sleep up there."

"So you walked," says Tubby.

I nod.

"Now help me here," he says, scratching the back of his head with the pen. "You walk up there, which makes it—what?

Maybe seven o'clock, if you're walking real slow. So how do we get a call about someone falling off a cliff at almost midnight?"

"Don't know," I say.

"What were you doing between seven and midnight?"

"Nothing."

"You musta been doing something."

I don't say anything.

"Or maybe you weren't up on Signal Hill all that time. Maybe you were off with somebody—your uncle maybe, or Frankie Walsh—grabbing a bite to eat. Well?"

"I wasn't. I was by myself, up by the tower, just looking at everything. The city, the lights coming on, the ocean coming in through the rocks."

Tubby lets out a big sigh. "So. You're sitting up there, taking in the sights. In the dark. In the cold. So how'd you end up over the cliff?"

"It's a bit fuzzy."

"Sounds it," says Tubby. "But think hard."

"I guess I was hungry, because I never had any supper. So I went for a little walk to take my mind off of it. That's when I musta fallen."

"You went for a walk and fell off a cliff?"

"It was foggy…"

"So foggy you couldn't see more'n a foot or two in front of you?"

"That's right," I say.

"Made everything invisible, I guess."

"Yup."

"So tell me," he says. "How'd somebody manage to see you fall off the cliff, in the middle of all that fog?"

Soon as I hear it, I think that's a good question. So good that I start to think maybe I figured Tubby for being a bit dumber than he really is. There's no good answer to that question.

He asks again, "Maybe you didn't hear. If it was so foggy you fell off a cliff, how could anybody who wasn't right beside you see it happen?"

I feel my face getting hot, but I can't think of anything to say.

Then, just when I figure he'll start really pushing me, he snaps his notebook shut. Just like that. Snaps it shut, puts it in his pocket and gives me a long, long look, right in the eyes.

"That's it for now," he says, finally breaking off the stare. "I got everything I need."

Then he's off down the hallway, with Dezzy letting out a giant sigh soon as he's gone.

"Sorry about that," he says. "But better to let him ask his questions while Ms. Puddister and I are here, rather than him hauling you off to the police station. Anyway, that's out of the way, so on to a happier topic."

He sits down on the end of the bed.

"Charlie," he says, "I got a proposition: how'd you like to come live with me. Just for a bit."

I don't know what to say to that.

"I mean, you've had a rough few weeks, with your dad, and now this"—he gives my cast a look—"so I just thought you might like to spend a few days out at my place, with my wife and me. Just while we're waiting for a foster home. I've got a nice place, with a yard. No kids, but I think you'd like it. And like I say, it wouldn't be forever—just till we get something sorted with a more permanent home. What do you say?"

"I don't know."

"I know it's unexpected. I didn't really think of it myself until a couple of days ago. And it's not something you have to do. You could come out and have a look at the place first if you want."

"And if I didn't like it?"

Dezzy looks over at Miz, who starts talking. "We'd have no choice but to send you back to the training school in White Hills."

"No way. I'm not going back there."

"Maybe the Waterford Hospital?" she asks, looking over at Dezzy.

"The Mental?" I say. "No—not there either. Not The Hollow. Not the Mental."

I look up at Dezzy.

"Your house," I say. "That'd be okay. For now."

Dezzy gives a smile and looks over at Miz.

"Good. Ms. Puddister has some paperwork for us to sign, and I'll find a doctor to sort out your discharge."

He stops in the doorway. "I think you'll like my place. It's quiet, right by the ocean—a neat spot for a kid from Alberta. It's even got a neat name. Quidi Vidi."

EIGHTEEN

I can just see Clare's house from the room I'm in.

"Your room," Dez called it when he opened the door. Except I don't want to call it that. Not that it's a bad room—in fact, it's the nicest room I ever had. Big old bed with a nice mattress that doesn't sag in the middle. A bookcase stuffed with books—mostly boring stuff like *Child Development: The Case for Early Intervention*. A desk with a computer on it—but not one that's hooked up to the Internet, since Dez says he just uses it for writing on. I figure this room is really his office, since there's a phone in it, but it's still a pretty nice bedroom. It just isn't mine, and I don't want to call it that, because as soon as a foster family comes up I'll be shipped out to Mount Pearl or wherever there's somebody willing to take in an orphan kid from Alberta.

Anyways, I can just see Clare's house from here. It's on the other side of the little bit of ocean that comes right into the middle of Quidi Vidi. I want to go over there because she still has my backpack. Unless Nick took it with him, which I don't think he did, because the cops might come looking for it. I'd like to get it, mostly because of that old T-shirt of my dad's, plus my jeans.

That's about all I got left of my old life, the only proof I ever lived in Fort Mac. Like, look at me now—I got new jeans Dez bought me because they had to cut the old pair off in the ambulance. New shirt, new underwear, new socks, all of it bought in St. John's. What's left from when my dad was alive, except what's in my head? I guess maybe that's how it is when you grow up—stuff from your old life keeps disappearing. It gets chucked in the garbage or gets left in a cupboard some-wheres or it ends up in the red bin for secondhand clothes. But me, I'm not really ready to have all that stuff ripped out from me, so I would like to go over to Clare's and get that back-pack back, just to have that stuff in my hands. To feel it. To give it a sniff and smell what things used to be like.

Except I can't really just walk over to Clare's and ask for it, for a couple of reasons. First, half the time Tubby is sitting out in front of Dez's in a cop car—not one painted up like a cop car, but a ghost car. Which anybody older than five can tell is a cop car right away, so why do they even bother pretending it's not? If I was making a ghost car I'd buy the most beat-up old piece of junk I could find, like a banged-up old Pontiac, and stick a fast engine in it. Then you'd see a ghost car. Course, maybe they do that already and they got ghost cars out there that are so ghosty that I don't even know they're there, but I doubt it. I don't think the cops are that smart. Anyways, Tubby isn't for sure, 'cause he's sitting out there in his 2005 Chevrolet Impala with the plain rims and dark blue paint and little antenna on the back that practically shouts out, "I'm a cop car. With a cop sitting in me."

So I can't just walk over to Clare's with him sitting there. Plus, let's say I did get over there, and I rang the bell and Clare's mom or dad answered. What am I going to say? Excuse me, I think you have some stuff I left here when my crazy murderer-uncle was chasing me outta your house while your daughter was having a beer? I don't think so. What I should do is phone, but when I look up Dalton in the phone book, there's about a hundred of them: Alfie, Arlene, Earl, Edith, Isaac, William...I have to cut down the number of possible Daltons, which I do by asking Dez what the street across the way is called.

"Quidi Vidi Road," he says, which has just one Dalton on it: Dalton, T. J. I decide to call at 4:30 PM when Clare should be home from school, but before her mom and dad get back from work. The clock hits 4:30, but I'm too scared, so I promise that I'll call when it hits 4:37. Which I do.

"Hello," says a girl.

"Clare?"

"Who's this?" she asks. She takes in a bit of a sniffle.

"It's me. Charlie."

"Charlie." She snuffs in again. "Sorry. I've got a cold—runny nose."

"'Kay."

She snuffs again. "Are you still in the hospital? I read you had that accident."

"No. I got out yesterday."

"So where are you?"

"I'm staying at Dez's—a guy who works with Child Services. I'm staying with him for a bit."

"That's nice."

"Funny thing is, it's just over from you—in Quidi Vidi."

The phone goes quiet.

"Clare?"

"Where? Which house?"

"A blue one—with a white fence in front. I can just see the top floor of your place from here."

"Really," says Clare. She doesn't sound too excited.

"Yeah. Anyways, I wondered if I could come over and pick up my stuff."

"Your stuff?"

"My backpack that I left…"

"Right, right, right," says Clare. "Listen, Charlie. You say you're living with somebody who works for the government?"

"Child Services."

"Right. Well, I don't think it would be a good idea for you to come over here right now. You haven't told anyone you were here, have you?"

"No."

"Good. I don't think the cops know anything about you being here, which is how I'd like to keep it. So, listen. Let me bring your stuff to you, 'stead of you coming here."

"Okay."

"There's an old shed down at the water, just past the brewery. That's the big green building. You can probably see it from where you are."

"I see it."

"We can meet down there tonight—after supper. My parents have got some dinner or something in town. Can you be there at seven?"

"I think so—I mean, I'd have to check with Dez."

"Just tell him you want to go for a walk. Can you walk?"

"Yeah. I'm slow, but I can. Doctor says I should, so Dez might like that."

"Good. It'll be dark, but just give a knock and I'll let you in. I've got some candles. Gerald and I used to hang out there when we were kids. Nobody else'll be around. We can talk, and I can give you your stuff. So right after supper, okay?"

"Okay."

She hangs up before I do.

A fog horn's blowing when I step outside after supper. I like it. I don't know why—I guess it makes things less lonely. I mean, the fog horn's blowing so people on ships can hear it, so you know other people are around, even if you can't see them.

I never saw fog before I moved here, only read about it or saw it in movies. And before I saw it, I just sorta thought of it as being a big lump of gray stuff that sits in one place, like a giant cotton ball dropped on your head. But when you're actually out in it, it's almost like it's alive or something, swirling around, brushing against your face, leaving drops on your hair. And then it might just float off completely, so everything's clear again. It's like something alive, creeping along, slipping over and under and around you. I like it, even if it did send me over that cliff.

Dez, he didn't like it so much when I asked him about going for a walk after supper.

"By yourself?" he asked.

"If that's okay—I been inside all day."

"Fog's coming in," he said, getting up to look for Tubby. He's not there though—must be suppertime.

"I guess it's okay. Just watch for cars. And don't be too long. Back by seven thirty?"

"Okay," I said, then headed off.

You know what I'm hoping? I know it's stupid, but I'm hoping Clare maybe wanted to meet at the shed so we'd be alone. And if that's how it is, I'm going to kiss her—not on the lips, unless she wants to, but on the cheek. Just to let her know I like her. Which, I know, is pretty stupid, since I'm only thirteen and she's, like...I don't know how old, really. Fifteen or sixteen? I'm not much good at guessing ages of people older than me—kind of like trying to figure out how far something is away from you. Maybe Clare is eighteen, but I don't think so. She doesn't seem that old—at least she didn't when I first met her, back at The Hollow. Now that I've seen her drinking a beer, and with that pill bottle in her hand, she does seem older.

Still, she looks like I could talk to her about whether she likes to draw pictures or what books she reads or what she does in the summer, so you never know—maybe she could like me. And if she did, maybe she'd kiss me back. Though probably I'm crazy for even thinking about it, I know. Which I can't stop doing.

Anyways, there's the shed, a little ways down a dirt path, off toward the water. There's no streetlight to show the way, though there is a bit of light flickering behind one of the windows—a candle, I guess. I tap at the door, pushing it open at the same time and calling, "Clare?"

Right away I see there's two people inside, huddled up together on the floor, away from the candle, off in the black. Soon as I step in they pull apart, and one—Clare—stands up and into the candlelight.

"Charlie," she says. "Jesus—you're quiet as a cat. What were you doing, sneaking up on us?"

"No. Didn't know there'd be anyone else in here—just you, I thought."

"Don't worry, Cowboy, it's just me," comes another voice. Frankie. "What are ya at?" he asks, giving me a nod.

"Good," I say. I still don't know how to answer that question.

"Jesus, some cast, b'y," he says. He comes closer and gives it a knock with his knuckles. I can smell beer on him, and probably Clare, too, since there's a few cans on the floor.

Clare moves her hand across her face a couple of times, pulling hair outta her eyes, I guess, though it's all done up in a ponytail, just like I thought it would be when I was thinking about her in the afternoon. I see strands of it are hanging down as she moves closer to the candle, reaching for something on the floor.

"Here," she says, holding up my backpack. "Everything's in it."

"My uncle looked through it," I say, reaching into it to feel around. "Seems like everything's here though."

"I'm sorry," says Clare. She looks like she means it. Then she puts her hand up to her mouth and gives a little cry.

"It's okay," I say. "Everything's here."

"It's not that I'm sorry about…"

"That's right, Charlie, b'y," comes a voice from behind me. "Poor young Clare's feeling bad about setting up this meeting we're about to have, isn't that right, Clare?"

It's Nick, standing two feet from me, blocking the door.

He reaches into his jacket pocket, then tosses something to Clare. A pill bottle.

"There you go, my girl," he says. "As promised. And yours, Frankie, is out on the path. Don't drink it all at once or it'll be the death of ya."

Clare doesn't look at me as she walks toward the door, but Frankie stops.

"We'll be right outside, Cowboy," he says. "Nick just wants to talk with ya—if he tries anything, just sing out and I'll be here quicker'n shit through a goose. All right?"

Then he follows Clare outside.

"Jesus, Charlie," Nick says, shutting the door behind them. "It hurts my feelings, that does—the way Clare gets all weepy and sorry 'bout settin' up this little meetin' between me and thee. 'Sorry, Charlie,' boo-hoo, like she's deliverin' ya to the devil himself. And here she was yesterday, beggin' me to give her a lend of those pain pills of mine. 'Cept she didn't have no money, Charlie, so what did she do? She begs me to work out a deal with her, find a way she could get ahold a some pills. Which I done, outta the kindness of my heart.

"'All right, girl,' I says, 'You just find me a quiet place to have a chat with me nephew,' I says, 'and I'll get ya a few of these Oxy-whatevers.' So we done our deal, like reasonable people. And here I come to find her cryin' 'bout how sorry she is to have done it. Jesus, you'd think I were out to slit yer throat, wouldn't ya, Charlie? Wha?"

There's a crate on the floor beside him that he kicks my way.

"Put your arse on that and we'll have a little talk."

He pulls an old chair with a busted back outta the corner, sitting in it right in front of the door.

"Now, me and thee had a little deal, too, didn't we, Charlie?"

He gives me a long stare, and I can see wheels moving behind his eyes, even if he's saying nothing, which is what I say too.

It's still and quiet till there's a knock at the door.

"You okay, Charlie?" Frankie calls.

Nick gives a little smile at that and stays quiet for another sec, then all at once whips his claw round and bashes it into the door as hard as he can. There's a snapping sound I think must be his hand till he swings it back into the candlelight and I see a long splinter sticking out of a claw from the wooden door. He takes hold of the splinter in his good fingers, looks at me and pulls it out.

"Don't feel nothing in that hand," he says, his eyes flickering black and orange in the candlelight.

He smiles again, turns to the door and shouts, "Leave us be," before turning round to me again.

"Now, we was talking about our deal. Which was that I'd go for the fire boys, up on the hill, and you'd give me the key. So..."

He holds out the claw and clicks the two fingers together, keeping his eyes on mine, like he's seeing right inside me.

"So give it to me," he says, dropping his voice to a whisper that slinks into my ear. "Go on, now, Charlie. Kick off that shoe, dig it out and give it to me. I means it. Either that or I'll look meself. And if I don't find it there, I'll—"

"Okay," I say. "I gotta stand up, though, with this cast."

"Stay where you're to," says Nick, and he bends forward in the chair and takes my foot in his hand. He unties the laces and slips it off and passes it to me. Then sits back and holds the claw out again. I take the insole out, wet and stinky, then tip the sneaker up till the key drops into my hand. I pass it to Nick. It's gold in the candlelight, sitting on his black palm. He holds it up, close to his eye, and squints at the number.

"What's that say, at the top?"

"One fifty-eight," I say, with Nick saying the numbers just behind me, like they're words to a song he sang a long time ago.

"One fifty-eight," he says again. "That's it, b'y. That's the key."

I expect him to tuck it somewheres safe—his shirt, his jeans—but he doesn't. 'Stead, he leaves it in his open palm, then offers it back to me.

"Go on," he says, holding the claw out, the key there for me to take. "Go on—take it. It's yers."

"Mine?"

"Well," says Nick, "yer old man's. But he's dead and gone now, so it's yers. Take it."

"But I thought…"

"What? That I wanted the key? No, b'y. The keys no good to me. What I wants is what that key can unlock. And the only person who can do that, Charlie, b'y, is you."

"I don't understand," I say, reaching out to take it. Nick's hand is dry and cold and hard as a rock when my fingers brush it.

"Course you don't," says Nick. "I knows that, so I'll explain it to ya. But first…"

He leans forward on the chair, an elbow on his knee, his claw reaching out to tap on my cast.

"But first I got to know if you're prepared to help me."

"Prepared? What do you mean 'prepared'?"

He leans back. "Well, what do I mean?"

He gives his chin a rub with the claw, *scritch-scratch* in the dark.

"I means this," he says at last. "Take yer little friend, Clare, there. Now there's a girl what I never even met till a few days ago, but right away I can tell she needs help. She's all messed up on those drugs. She's in and outta rehab like a fly at a shit pot. Got no one what loves her. Leastways, that's how she feels, with her parents off travelin' the world all the time. Sure they're planning a trip right now—off to New York or some such—and her just outta the rehab. It's not right, b'y. And she knows it's not right."

"How'd you know all this stuff?"

"Gerald," says Nick. "Me and him and Frankie been talking a bit lately. I'm giving them a hand getting a bit of a business started, using some old friends of mine. So we've had a chat or two. Anyways, that's a girl what's in need of help. Anyone can see it. So I been helpin' best I can, gettin' a few Oxys now an' again—just while she's going through this rough patch. Checkin' up on her when she's home alone, her parents off to the movies or dinner or wherever. Couple a nights ago, they spent half the night at some fancy spot downtown, their just-home daughter left all alone. Can you believe that, Charlie? It's a sin, b'y."

He leans back for a second.

"Speaking of sins," he says, "I'm goin' to have a draw if ya don't mind."

He pulls out a smoke and bends into the candle to light it, the scar down his face white like wax on his cheek.

"Now," he says, blowing the smoke outta the corner of his mouth, away from my face, which he's leaning into again.

"That's what I means by help, with Clare—doing the right thing, even though I don't got to do nothing. I mean, she's nothin' to me—not my sister, not my daughter. Nothing. But I feels the need to do what I can. Because, you know, Charlie, she's right on the edge, b'y. One little shove the wrong way and she'd be over. I'm talkin' about doin' herself some harm— doin' away with herself, like. And nobody in the world would be surprised if she turned up in the Gut one mornin', floatin' facedown, done in by an overdose of those Oxys."

"You wouldn't…," I start.

"Whoa now, mister," says Nick, holding up his hand. "Don't you go readin' nothin' into what we're talkin' 'bout here. I'm talkin' 'bout helpin' people—not doin' them a mischief. Jesus, Charlie—you and yer imagination. You should be ashamed."

He takes a long pull on the smoke, then stubs it out on his palm and drops it onto the shed floor.

"Jesus. Why does people always think the worst of me? Why is that, Charlie?"

"I don't know," I say, looking at the cigarette that's still smoldering on the floor.

"Anyways, see what I means about Clare—'bout how I'm helpin' her, just because it's the right thing to do? And that's why I wants you to help me. Not because I'm yer uncle, nor because you got the fear of God put into ya about me because of what some social workers told ya I done years ago. I wants you to help me because it's the right thing to do. To help a man what needs some help, after doin' twenty hard years inside. You'd be givin' me a hand up by helpin' me—makin' it easier for me to take care of meself, to get my own place, to hold my head up when I walks down Duckworth Street. To get back a bit of the pride what got splattered all over walls of three friggin' prisons—'scuse me for swearing."

"That's okay."

"Swears a bit yourself, do ya, Charlie?"

"Not really. But I heard it lots."

"No doubt ya did, with yer old man," says Nick. He gives me a wink.

"My dad didn't swear...much," I say. Which is true. Sometimes when he was drinking he'd swear, which I didn't like because it was always angry then. But sometimes it wasn't, like when we'd be out together doing something— maybe fishing, say—and he'd swear about "the god-damned fish, hiding up their own arseholes." And he'd be smiling after he said it—and giving me a wink too.

"He only swore sometimes."

"Well," says Nick, "guess he were a reformed character out there in Alberta. Good for him, I says. New province, new life. Good for him."

He pulls out another smoke and lights it.

"And ya know something, Charlie? He'd want you to do the right thing by me too."

Nick's waiting for me to say something, but I don't.

"He really would. That's why he were comin' out here—to get me my stuff what's locked up with that key. So, you give me a hand here—you help me out—and you're doing right by yer old man. Fulfilling his dyin' wish, ya might say."

He takes a long drag.

"So, b'y—whaddaya say? You wants to do the right thing?"

I do—I do want to do the right thing. But right now, I don't know what the right thing is. In fact, the only thing I'm sure of is that Nick really might hurt Clare if I don't help him. He already killed two guys, so what's a kid to him? And he's right—nobody'd think anything about it if some sad girl ended up drowning herself with her stomach full of those pills. I think of that, of somebody finding Clare in the water, floating in her blue jeans and her brown jacket. Think of her getting hauled outta the water and some paramedic wearing blue rubber gloves pulling her hair back to look close at her face. And her getting put in an ambulance that comes without any sirens going. No sirens for people to listen for, to look up from their tables and wonder what's happening. Then at the hospital her parents come in and see her, and they don't even get to brush her hair outta her face one last time because somebody wearing blue rubber gloves already did that.

I see all that—like a dream that happens in a second, looking at Nick, him looking at me. "Okay," I say. "I'll help you."

"Right on, b'y," says Nick, and he gives my cast a couple of taps with the claw.

"Good man. Now listen."

He leans in as close as he can get. "This key, it opens a safety deposit box what belonged to yer old man."

"In Fort McMurray?"

"No, here, in St. John's. He had it years ago, before he ever thought of going west. He's paid the rent on it for all them years, and kept the key close, for when the time came."

"The time for what?"

"For when I got out, see? There's something in that box what belongs to me."

"And my dad was gonna give it to you?"

Nick nods, with a smile. "Now yer getting it, b'y. That's right. Something that he was gonna give to me. Except now, he ain't here to give it, is he?"

I shake my head.

"And that's a problem," Nick says. "Because only the person what rents the box is allowed to open it."

"But what about when they die?"

"Exactly," says Nick, snapping the fingers on his good hand. "When someone dies and don't leave a will or nothing, only immediate family gets to open the box. Which is you."

"'Kay," I say. "So I can go to the bank and open this box…"

"It's not simple," says Nick. "You're not a grown-up yet—how old are ya? Ten?"

"I am not ten," I say. "I am thirteen. Almost fourteen."

"Course you are," says Nick. "Thirteen. Getting old, but even so, not so old as to open up a safety deposit box without the approval of yer guardian—he or she what's looking after you. Legal, like."

"Dez," I say.

"Right again," says Nick.

"But Dez isn't going to let me go to a bank and take something out to give to you."

"No, he's not. But he will let ya put something in."

I laugh.

"Me? Put something in? What have I got to put in?"

"Ashes," says Nick.

"My dad?"

Nick nods. "His ashes. From the urn. I seen it at the funeral home."

"But I don't have that—that urn."

"No, but you can get it. They're not going toss it out, even if it is a Sykes. It's up on a shelf somewhere, waiting for you to collect it. When you're ready. So you tell Dez you're ready. Now. And he'll get it for ya."

"But ready to put it in a safety deposit box?"

"Sure," says Nick. "Proper thing for something as valuable as ashes. Not all of them mind—just a bit of them, in an envelope or something. Just tell Dezzy ya had a bad dream about them ashes gettin' blowed away in a storm or washed away in a flood, and ya wants to set a few of them aside in a safe place. And ya knows about his safety deposit box yer old man had back when he were young."

"But the key—he's going to think that's weird."

"He's not going to think anything about. He's not some cop, always thinkin' the worst a people. He's a social worker, always thinkin' everybody's good, deep down. So ya got a key to a safety deposit box what belonged to yer old man.

What odds? He'll just go down to the bank, check to see it's true, then sign ya in."

"And what? Watch me open the thing up?"

"No. He'll just sign ya in as yer guardian. Then you goes into a little room, all by yerself, an' they gives ya the box."

"Okay."

"Okay," says Nick. "So, inside there'll be a letter—an envelope—sent to an old aunt, Esther Sykes. It'll be stamped from Trepassey, with a date on it: September 17, 1989. That's what I wants."

"You mailed it. After the murder."

Nick's face scrinches up tight.

"How'd you know about that?"

"Dez," I lie. "Dez told me about it—what happened back then."

"Did he?" says Nick. "Well, don't believe everything Dezzy tells ya."

I nod.

"But yer right," he says. "I sent it off to the old aunt, for yer dad to have. An' it's got something in it what belongs to me."

"But if you sent it to my dad, isn't it his?"

Nick puts his burnt hand on my cast, a claw on each side of my leg.

"Yer helpin' me on this, Charlie, am I right?"

His claw slips onto the cast, the fingers pinching together.

"So take my word on it. It belongs to me. Not to yer old man, not to you, not to Dezzy. To me. Understand?"

I nod. Nick's fingers are starting to dig into the cast, making my leg shake, even if I don't feel anything through the plaster.

"So," he says, squeezing harder, "you see that letter, you takes it out, you put some of them ashes in the safety deposit box, an' you shoves that letter down inside that cast, where nobody can see. And then ya leaves with Dez and go get a milkshake or an ice cream or whatever the frig he wants to do to make ya feel better after this sorry occasion. Right? Then I'll come and find ya, and you give me the letter. Understand?"

I swallow and nod.

"I wants to hear ya say it, Charlie. Do you understand what I'm telling ya?"

"I understand."

"Good," says Nick, letting go of my cast.

Later, back in the bedroom at Dezzy's, I see there's two dents in the cast, deep and black where Nick had hold of me. I scrub till the plaster starts to crumble, but the stains, they don't come out.

NINETEEN

Next day everything happens like Nick said it would. I tell Dez I want to put some of my dad's ashes in a safety deposit box my dad had, and he says sure. He says he can call the bank and arrange that. Then that night he brings home the urn. It's a wood box, sanded smooth and colored a dark reddy-brown. It's the size of a Kleenex box, but heavier when Dez passes it to me.

"You want some time alone?" he says. "In your room?"

I have to think about what to say to that, because we're downstairs in the living room with the *Simpsons* on the TV. I guess Dez is thinking that maybe this little moment when he passes my dad's ashes over to me, maybe having Homer and Bart fighting in the background isn't quite right—that maybe I feel like crying or something. But you know what? I don't feel like crying, because it doesn't feel like I just been handed my dad. It just feels like I've been handed a nice box. I know my dad's ashes are in it, but that's not my dad. Next morning we go to the bank. Just like Nick said, Dez signs a piece of paper, a teller takes the key and I follow her to a little room behind a big steel door—a vault. Teller's not that pretty, but she's got a nice skirt on and a nice shape, which I can't help noticing, even though I'm carrying my dad's ashes and I'm supposed to be getting a letter to give to my murderer uncle. Even with all that going on I'm wondering what kind of underwear the woman walking in front of me is wearing. Anyways, Teller isn't real pretty, but she does have a nice shape when she's walking in front of you.

"Can I have the key, please, Charlie?" she says. Then she goes to a wall full of little compartments and unlocks one and pulls out a long, thin metal box.

"Follow me," she says, and we walk down to another little room with a table and two chairs. She sits the box down and pulls out a chair for me, while I set the urn beside the box.

"That must hurt," she says, looking at my cast, before she spins the box round to face me.

"Just flip up this clip," she says, "and pull the top back, okay?"

"'Kay."

"And ring that bell when you're done."

She points to an old-timey silver bell on the table.

Then I'm alone.

I pull hard on the lever and the whole top swings open, with the letter sitting on top, like somebody put it there yesterday. *Ester Sykes* is written on it in pencil, with an address underneath: *Harmony Court, St. John's*. And that's it.

No return address, no postal code, nothing. Just those six words in pencil, written slow and hard, I'd say, seeing how thick the black marks are. There's some other stuff in the box: two sets of car keys and a see-through plastic bag of some powdery stuff, yellowy white, which I don't want to know what it is. There's not much in the letter by the feel of it—just a piece of paper I can't read, even when I hold it up to the light.

Should I open it? It's been opened before—I guess by my dad—because it's torn on the back. But somebody taped it all up—my dad, likely too. So I could open it again and see what's inside and nobody'd ever know I did it. I could just hand it over to Nick and tell him it was like that when I got it. How'd he know any different? Except he might. And let's say there is some crazy secret thing in there and he figures I read it. Then he might slit my throat or make me swallow a bunch of pills or haul me up a cliff and toss me over. And what could I do about it? Run away with my leg in a cast? Whack him over the head with a crutch? Better safe than sorry, I figure. And stupid. Better safe, stupid and alive than smart, sorry and dead.

I take the letter out and slip it down into my cast. I'm just about to stand up when I remember I'm supposed to put some ashes in there—in the metal box, in an envelope Dezzy gave me. But all of a sudden I don't feel like it. I'll put Dezzy's envelope in, but no ashes. A long metal box locked up inside another metal box doesn't seem like a place for much of anything, even ashes. I stick Dezzy's empty envelope in the safety deposit box and leave the urn closed. No one's going to look inside either one of those boxes, except me.

I close the box and leave it right beside me on the table so Teller will have to lean in close to me to pick it up. I feel kind of creepy doing it, but I do it anyway. Then I ring that bell and think about those dogs Pavlov had while I wait for Teller to walk in and lean close.

TWENTY

"That was tough," Dez says when we leave the bank. "With the ashes."

"Guess so."

"Good idea, though, putting some in a safe place. The rest you can scatter in a nice spot when you're older. Plenty of time to figure that out. For now"—he puts his hand on my back—"let's get a bit of a treat. How about a chocolate croissant?"

"Never had one."

"Auntie Crae makes the best—store's right across the street."

"Could I maybe just sit outside for a bit? It's nice in the sun."

Dez gives a look up the street and spots Tubby, sitting in his not-so-secret cop car. He trots up and comes back a minute later.

"All right," he says. "You sit while I grab us something to eat."

I nod and sit on a metal bench in front of the bank. It's painted black and it's hot, but it feels nice after being in the little room with no windows. Today seems like the first sunny day since me and my dad left Alberta, and when I close my eyes and let the world go all red under my lids, I can feel the heat slipping in through my jacket and my track pants, which is what I have to wear with this big cast on. It feels good and sleepy, which is a funny way to feel when you're sitting on a bench on a downtown street and you can hear people talking and walking close by. It's a floaty feeling, and I like it. I can pretend I'm back in Fort Mac, sitting outside school on an afternoon in June when school is almost out for summer, waiting for my dad to drive me home…

Someone sits down beside me. It's Clare.

"Hi ya," she says. "Can I sit for a sec?"

"Sure," I say, looking round.

"It's okay. It's just me—no Frankie. No Nick. That an urn?"

I nod.

"With your dad's ashes?"

I nod again.

"Figured."

She looks sad.

"You okay?" I say.

"Not really. I got busted last night."

"Busted?" I say. I look up the street at Tubby's car.

"By my parents," says Clare. "They came home early from whatever they were doing and found me on the couch, nodded out."

She bites her lip, white spreading round where her teeth are pressing.

"Friggin' pill bottle was still in my hand."

"Was Frankie with you?"

Clare shakes her head. "No. Frankie was off with Nick. They got something going with Gerald—buying stuff, selling stuff. DVDs or iPods. Stolen, probably. I don't care. I'm outta here anyway."

"Whaddaya mean?"

"Back to rehab."

"When?"

"Tomorrow. Lunchtime, I guess. Whenever my dad can drive me out there. Till then, I gotta stay with Dad."

"Where's he now?"

Clare nods at the bank.

"Back there—that's his branch. That's how I saw you just now. Dad made me come to work with him this morning, and I saw you and that guy leaving."

"Dez."

"Figured. Anyways, I saw you and I just wanted to talk to you for a sec. To say I'm sorry. About Nick and stuff—letting him know you were meeting me in the shed."

"It's okay. I don't blame you for anything. I mean, Nick, he's a scary guy."

"I wasn't scared though," says Clare. "Not of him anyways."

"What *were* you scared of?"

She's quiet for a long time—both of us are just sitting, watching people walk past talking on their cell phones, stuffing some breakfast thing in their mouths, rushing along to make it somewhere on time.

"What scared you, Clare?" I ask again.

She looks at me and I can see she is crying now—tears, big ones. Sometimes when I cry my dad would wipe them off my cheeks. Not always. Sometimes he'd get mad and tell me to stop. But sometimes he'd brush them off. I want to brush off Clare's. But I don't.

"The feeling," she says.

"What feeling?"

"Oh, Charlie," she says, with a little laugh. "It's just a feeling. It's hard to talk about."

She waits a good bit, sniffling.

"It's a feeling like I'm living inside a long, long line of Wednesday afternoons in February. They stretch out forever—all those Wednesday afternoons, all the same. No leaves, no flowers, no colors, just gray. I look down that line of days and it's..."

She shrugs.

"Empty," I say. "A void."

She turns to me, lifts up her eyebrows. Her eyes are wide and green and wet, likes leaves after it rains in the spring.

"A void," she says. "Going on forever. You feel that?"

"Sometimes," I say. "Except with me, it's not like a tunnel. It's a hole, with nothing at the bottom, and me right on the edge with nothing to keep me out."

More people go past. They look happy in the sun, taking their jackets off, putting on sunglasses. It's funny to see everybody happy just a couple of feet away, while me and Clare talk about what we're talking about. There must be a better word for it than funny, but I don't know what it is. But I bet there is one, just meant to describe how funny this feels, to be sad, a couple of feet away from everybody else's happy.

"Clare," I say after a bit. "Do those pills—do they make the feeling go away?"

She wipes her cheek.

"They used to, for a bit, but now I feel ten times worse when it comes back…"

She stops and takes a snuffle in.

"No," she says. "They don't make it go away."

She sighs a big sigh.

"I just wanted to say sorry—about how things worked out with your uncle. Setting you up like that for some pills. It was wrong."

"It's okay."

"It's not," she says. "But I did it and I'm sorry. Anyways…"

She reaches into her jean's pocket. Her fingers move inside, feeling for something. I bet they're warm.

"I wanted to give you this."

She pulls out a cell phone and passes it to me.

"Just for now—while I'm inside. We're not allowed to have them. It's got a phone book in it"—she shows me how to scroll down—"with lots of numbers. Gerald, Frankie—Dez is in there too. I put his number in when you called the other day. Is he a nice guy?"

"Guess so. He's getting me a chocolate croissant from over there."

"They're good," says Clare. "Dad used to get them for me on Saturdays."

She looks like she's gonna start crying again.

"Anyway, Charlie, I gotta go. Dad'll be calling the cops if I don't go back inside. So you take care, okay?"

All of a sudden she scrinches over to me and gives me a kiss on the cheek. Her lips touch me just for a sec, but they're soft and warm and make me think of the sun, yellow and hot.

"Bye," she says, then runs back inside the bank.

I look after her for a long while. I don't want to move in case I might forget how her lips feel on my cheek. I'm still looking when the claw creeps along my shoulder, then fastens itself round the back of my neck.

"That's a nice girl, giving you a kiss like that," Nick says as he sits beside me. "I means it—she really is nice. And don't you go thinking otherwise, Charlie. Don't you go thinking she set ya up again for a meeting with me, because she had nothing to do with me finding you here—not a thing, b'y. Did that all on my own. So don't blame her."

"What do you want?" I say. I look up the street for Tubby and his car, but it's gone, empty curb where it was just a minute ago.

"You knows what I want, Charlie," says Nick. He slips his claw down on my arm and squeezes me tight to him.

"So let's go to the car I borrowed from a friend over here," he pulls me to my feet and leads me into an alley beside the bank. "And ya can give it to me."

It's Gerald's car, the big blue one we took out to Cape Spear. That time I sat in the backseat, but now I'm up front, where Nick shoves me when he yanks the door open.

"Stay put," he says. "We're off for a little drive."

He starts heading outta town, out into all that scrub and little trees that start as soon as the traffic lights end. The road mostly goes right through all those little trees, but once in a while it swings out toward the ocean, blue and white off to the left. It looks cold and big and strong.

"Cops'll be looking for us," says Nick. "So I wants to put some miles between us and town."

"But they don't know I'm with you."

"They'll figure it out," says Nick. "Quick enough too. Even the RNC can get four from two and two—soon as they figure three and four ain't the right suspects."

Nick gives me a smile, but I don't smile back.

"Listen, Charlie, I ain't out to hurt ya. It's just that I needs ya to help me get back what's mine by rights."

"The letter?"

"The letter, b'y. The letter. Have ya got it?"

"Yeah."

"Good man. Hang on to it for another bit now—there's a gravel pit coming up just over this hill—or there was twenty years ago. We'll get off the road and have a bit of a chat."

A gravel pit doesn't sound like a very private place to me—a giant hole full of trucks and dozers and guys in hard hats. But this gravel pit isn't anything like that. It's a little gray gash cut into all the green little trees, with a pile of gravel off to one side. And that's it. No gate. No trucks. Nobody in a hard hat. Just a big pile of gravel, which Nick drives behind. He puts the car in Park and shuts off the engine, then turns to me and holds out the claw.

"The letter," he says.

I set the urn down on the floor of the car, then work the envelope out from my cast and pass it over.

He holds it between his fingers—holds it for a long time.

"Jesus Christ," he says at last. He runs his claw across the front, black fingers against black lines.

"Twenty years," he says.

He works a fingernail under the flap and slits it open with one slice and pulls out a piece of paper. He unfolds it and sets it on his leg. Then he laughs—a chuckle at first, to himself, then more laughing, louder and faster till the sounds all string together and it's a big belly laugh. There's even tears on his face—I see them on his cheek, running down that long scar he's got, till they hit his chin and hang in a salty ball.

"Ahh," he says, giving his chin a wipe. "Ahh, Jesus."

He turns to me and gives the paper a tap.

"Charlie, you know how many nights I lay awake, thinking of holding this in my hands?"

I take a closer look at the paper. It's old, with lines where's it's been folded, and a jagged edge on one side like it got ripped out of a notebook. There's writing at the bottom, and just above, covering half the page, is a map, in red pen, like a teacher would use.

"I dunno," I say.

"Thousands," he says. "Thousands of nights I lay in that cell, thinking of having my hands on this, and now here it is. Jesus."

He lights a cigarette, rolling down the window a crack to let the smoke out.

"Ah," he says again and gives his head a shake, smiling a smile that looks happy and sad at the same time.

"Charlie, b'y, there ain't many moments in life like this one. Like this one. Right here."

He takes another drag.

"Least not in my life."

A long wisp of smoke slips between his lips, stretching into a gray line that gets sucked out the window.

"And it's all down to you, Charlie. It were s'posed to be me and yer old man, but it couldn't be yer old man, so it had to be you. And you done it."

He holds out his good hand for me to shake. I do.

"Thanks," he says. And right when he says it, I know it's my chance.

"Now you owe me one," I say, still holding the hand.

Nick's smile changes a bit, turns down a bit, looks more serious a bit, but it's still there. He works the cigarette into it, holding my hand tight, me holding tight right back. And he gives a little nod.

"You're right, b'y. Now I owes you one." He lets go. "So whaddaya want?"

"The truth."

He gives a laugh. "And you think an old ex-con can give the truth about anything?"

"You can tell me the truth about that map—what it's to and what me and my dad were doing, coming out here with that key."

Nick flicks the smoke out the car window.

"The truth is I don't know what that map's to, exactly."

I don't take my eyes off his for a long time—long enough for his face to get blurry and start swimming. He looks away first, for a sec, then stares back.

"It's true," he says. "I don't know—for certain—what the map's to. I only know what I hope it's to. And that's money. Lots of it. But I don't know. Not for sure."

"But you know the other stuff," I say. "About me and my dad coming out here, why we were on that highway that night…"

"Hold up a minute, Charlie," says Nick. "I didn't kill yer old man."

"I didn't say you did. But you know the other stuff—what we were doing on that road, in that car. And I don't know the why about anything."

I'm talking loud, shouting, pretty much.

"I'm used to not knowing stuff," I say. "Stuff like why my mom died, or why my dad hated me sometimes. Not knowing how come we never had any cars in the driveway on Christmas and Easter when everybody else had their grammies and grampies and cousins and nieces and nephews, all in the driveway and in the backyard and on the back deck, smoking and playing and having a beer or a pop, but not me and my dad. Over at our place, it's always just me and him.

Except now it's only me. Why is that? I don't know. But I think maybe you do. So you owe me that."

For the first time since I met him, Nick looks scared, and just for a sec his eyes turn from drills to holes. Just for a sec.

"Jesus, Charlie, calm yerself, b'y. It's not just you, is it? You got yer uncle Nick now, sitting right across from ya."

"Why is that?" I say. "Why is it that all I got now is my uncle, sitting across from me in a car that's hiding from the police? You know the truth about that too, don't you?"

Nick nods. "I guess I do."

"So tell me. Tell me the truth."

Nick's claw scritches his chin.

"Okay," he says. "But remember this when I tells ya." He points the claw at me. "Remember the truth'll make us even. And it was you what wanted to know it."

TWENTY-ONE

Nick lights another cigarette and it all comes tumbling out with the smoke.

"I was seventeen when my parents died in a fire. Yer old man, Mikey, he were fifteen. We was out that night, down to the pool hall, when Dicky Thomas come rushing in, hollering 'bout half of Cook Street being alight, our place too. And so it was—the whole street lit up, you could see it from downtown soon as you turned up the hill for home—a glow, the clinkers falling as far down as Military Road."

Nick's cigarette flares red when he takes a big draw in.

"We seen that glow and started running, straight up Long's Hill. Me mom—your nan, Doreen—she died that night. Ceiling fell in on her. Dick, the old man, he died three days later. From burns, they told us, but I always figured it were the smoke he drawed in, trying to pull the old girl out from under. He wheezed something terrible them last three days, pulling air in and out so hard his breath sounded like a saw cutting old wood. Me and Mikey took turns sittin' with him, but he never opened his eyes. And then he were gone, just stopped breathing, and us not even able to hold his hand for all the bandages they had him wrapped in."

"How'd it start?" I ask.

"Dunno. Started two doors down, to the Ryans, and we never knowed why. Wires. Pennies in a fuse box. Smoking. Bad chimney. Fat in a pan unminded. Dunno. If the fire boys ever figured it out, they didn't bother telling a couple of orphans, which is what we was from that night on. Orphans, sent off to Cliffside. You heard about Cliffside, Charlie?"

"A bit."

"So you knows it were a bad place—for the little ones specially. Me and Mikey, we was too old for the Brothers to mess with by the time we went in, but the wee ones—what they did to some of them, it was a sin. And them Brothers supposed to be doing God's work on earth. Sure, it was the devil's work more like. Screaming at the little ones, making them drop their drawers for beatings. And the ones they took a fancy to—the ones they thought was too scared to say a word, or was crying out for a bit of kindness—they was the ones that got the worst of it. Taken behind closed doors, pawed at, felt up, raped, some of them."

The sun outside the car goes behind a cloud, and I can see it's going to turn gray, the wind kicking up dust in the gravel pit. All of a sudden I'm cold.

"Some of the Brothers was all right," says Nick. "Tough, but all right. But others. My god. They were the worst of what a man could be. Twisted little runts of things—never did a normal thing in their life—never went to a movie or kissed a girl, and them left in charge of a bunch of wee boys."

Nick takes a last pull on the smoke and flicks it out the window.

"That place was like a cart full of shit nobody gave a damn about cleaning up. So long as it stayed up there on that hill, behind them walls. Those poor little lonely kids, locked inside with those twisted bastards."

"And Brother Sullivan—the dead one—he was one of the bad ones?"

Nick gives a hard laugh. "He was a bad one, all right. He was one of the arseholes in charge of the place—a supervisor or something, figuring out who works where, who gets shipped off to another parish."

"He was hurting boys too?"

"It were the Brothers he were screwing," says Nick. "Blackmailing 'em. It were Mikey what found it out. I were outta Cliffside by then, living on my own in a boardinghouse over to Freshwater Road, but Mikey were still inside, sleeping on a ward.

"One night he hears some kid crying, somewheres off hidden behind a door, quiet. So he slips down the hall and listens till he finds where the sound's to: a closet where the janitor keeps his gear. Mikey opens the door and at first he don't see nothing, just some buckets and a mop. But the light from the hallway sparks off something bright tucked away in a corner. Eyes."

"Who's that?" Mikey says.

"Nobody," comes this voice.

"Well, Nobody," says Mikey, "you're found, b'y, so come on out."

"If I does," says the voice, "you won't hurt me, will ya?"

"Jesus," says Mikey, "who is that?"

"It's me," says the kid, crawling out from the corner on his hands and knees.

"Jesus, Weasel," says Mikey, seeing it's Walter Puddicombe, what everybody calls Weasel, because he's so small and quick. "What are ya doing, stuffin' yourself into the back of the broom closet?"

"Hidin'" he says.

"From who?"

"Can't say," says Weasel.

"Bullshit," says Mikey. "You're after waking me up with yer cryin', so you can tell me what it's about. C'mon, now, b'y, who'er ya hidin' from?"

"You won't tell?"

"Get on with it, Weasel."

"A Brother," he says.

"What Brother?"

Weasel starts to cry, standing there in his pajamas, rubbing his hands together, staring down at the floor.

"Jesus, Weasel," says Mikey, seeing the kid's scared shitless. Mikey flips on the light in the closet and steps inside, closing the door behind him. He grabs a bucket and flips it over so he can sit on it. "Now tell me what's going on."

So Weasel starts talkin', 'bout how one of the Brothers, Brother Alfred, he'd been comin' to Weasel's ward every couple of nights for mor'n a year—since before Mikey and me got sent up the hill. At first, Brother Alfred didn't try nothing, just sat beside him—"Tucking you in" he'd say. Then he lay down beside Weasel for a night or two, rubbing his back "to help you get to sleep." Not long after that, Brother started sticking his hands down Weasel's bottoms, feeling round for his bird. Weasel, he didn't like that, asked him to stop. But Brother Alfred kept coming back; he said it was all right and asked, didn't it feel good? Weasel said it didn't, said he didn't like it. But he figured he was too small to stop him, so it kept going on, even when Weasel'd pretend to be asleep. Then one night, Brother Alfred comes and wants Weasel to touch his bird. But Weasel, he won't do it. And he starts bawling so loud Brother figures the other kids might wake up, so he gets up and leaves. The next day Brother Alfred calls Weasel outta class and into the boys' bathroom on the third floor, which hardly anybody uses because the drains don't work right and it stinks like piss. And Brother Alfred, he tells Weasel that if he don't like what happened last night, maybe he'd like this better. Then he takes the wood pointer he's got and smacks him, hard as he can, on the back and on the arse, and on the back of his legs, hitting him so hard it leaves big bruises right through his clothes. It goes on for a long time, says Weasel, long enough that Brother Alfred is sweating at the end of it, his hair sticking to his forehead, his face all red.

"How does that feel?" says Brother, just before he gives Weasel a last whack and walks outta the bathroom, leaving him laying on the floor, crying. It's a week before Weasel can walk right. As soon as he can he does a runner, taking off to the Jungle—a place in the woods teenagers hang out at, down behind the mall. The cops, they figure that's where he's to, because he's done a couple of runners before and always ended up in the same place.

This time, though, he don't come quiet. 'Stead, he starts shouting 'bout how he ain't going back, not after what Brother done to him. The cops laugh at first, but they stop soon as he shows 'em the bruises on his legs. And this time, 'stead of taking him back to Cliffside, they drives him down to the cop shop and sit him in a room by himself. They leave him there for a long whiles, with nothing but a Mars bar and a warm orange pop to eat the whole time. Finally a cop in a suit and tie comes in and puts a pen and a pad of yellow paper on the table and asks Weasel about what happened to him—how he come to get those bruises on his legs. And Weasel, he tells everything: about the backrubs, the beatings, about getting felt up—everything, with the cop writing it all down, holding up his hand when he needs Weasel to slow down. Then he reads it back to Weasel and gets him to sign it. After that, he drives him back to Cliffside, with Sullivan there to meet them, soon as they step inside the orphanage.

"You go up to the ward, Walter. I'll speak with you later," says Sullivan, before him and the detective walk off to Sullivan's office. Weasel seen the detective snooping round a bit over the next couple a days, talking to a few other boys. But there weren't a sign of Brother Alfred—not until one night about a week after Weasel talked to the cops. It were late—gone midnight, Weasel figured. He were laying in bed, like he always done in those days, waiting to see if Brother Alfred was going to show up. And while he were laying there, looking out at the window across from his bed, he sees the shadows move like they do when a car pulls into the driveway. So Weasel, he gets up and creeps over to the window and has a look out. And who do he see but Brother Alfred, all bundled up in a big coat and carrying a suitcase, walking out to a taxi. Right behind him comes Sullivan, the two of them standing together for a bit, 'fore they shake hands. And Brother Alfred gets in the cab, with Sullivan trotting up the steps back into Cliffside.

"That's the last I seen of Brother Alfred," Weasel tells Mikey.

"So why you still hidin'?" Mikey asks.

"It ain't Brother Alfred I'm hidin' from now," says Weasel. "It's Brother Sullivan."

"Sullivan's been doing shit to you too?" says Mikey.

"It's not that," says Weasel. "It's what he's making me say."

"About what?" says Mikey.

"'Bout how the Brothers been abusing me," says Weasel.

"You mean he's making you say this stuff to the cops?" says Mikey.

Weasel shakes his head. "To the Brothers. He's making me say it right to the Brothers."

"I don't getcha," says Mikey. "When did all this start—all this talking to the Brothers?"

"Just after Brother Alfred left," says Weasel. "Right after that, Brother Sullivan, he calls me down to his office and says he heard about how Brother Alfred was doing bad stuff to me. Then he says he's heard stories that there might be other Brothers doing the same stuff to other kids. And he asks me if I heard any of them stories. So I said, Yeah, I did—everybody heard 'em. So he says to me, 'Well, Walter,' he says, 'I've got a plan to stop that from happening, but I needs your help.'

"What do I got to do?" Weasel says.

"In the next couple of days," says Sullivan, "I'll call you down to my office for a meeting with one of these bad Brothers. I'll ask you a couple of questions about the Brother, and you say yes. No more. Just yes. Understand?"

Weasel, he says he understands, but he don't really, because he got no idea what these questions is going to be about. But he finds out soon enough. A couple a nights later he gets told to go down to see Brother Sullivan in his office after supper. He goes in and sees Sullivan sitting at his desk, talking with Brother Burke, what nobody likes because he's always pinching the kids when they gets an answer wrong— hard enough to leave a bruise, too, sometimes.

"Now, Walter," says Brother Sullivan to Weasel. "Is this the man who abused you?"

Weasel ain't sure what to say to that, because if Sullivan means, is this the man what pinches you when you can't figure three into twenty-one, then yes, it is. But if he means is this the man what comes to him in the night, then it's no, because Brother Burke, he never done nothing like that to Weasel. Weasel's trying to figure it out when Sullivan says, "Remember our talk from this afternoon, Walter?"

Then he know the answer Sullivan wants, and he gives it to him. "Yes."

Brother Burke, he gets outta his chair, shouting what a damn lie that is, but before he can take a step toward Weasel, Sullivan gets between the two of them.

"Enough!" he shouts, putting his hand right in Brother Burke's face. Then he turns round to Weasel and says, soft and quiet, "Are you willing to sign a paper saying that, Walter?"

Weasel knows the answer to that too. "Yes."

Then Sullivan gives Weasel a little shove into the hallway and closes the door behind me.

"This happened more than once?" Mikey asks Weasel.

"Lots of times," says Weasel. "Sometimes it'd be Brothers I knowed, and sometimes it were Brothers I never seen before. Them was the worst—specially the last one—a Brother what looked like he mighta been one of the kids, he were so young. I come in and says my yes, and all of a sudden this Brother, he falls over, right there in Brother Sullivan's office, right onto the floor. It were after that I told Brother Sullivan I weren't going to do it no more, which he don't like. Except 'stead of yelling at me, which I can tell he wants to, he gets all nice and quiet, and starts talking 'bout how it's really God's work we're doing, protecting the boys from the bad Brothers.

"You wouldn't want to go against God's work, would you, Walter?" he says. "Anyone who does that suffers the flames of eternal Hell, Walter. And you don't want to spend eternity gnashing your teeth in hellfire, do you, Walter?"

Weasel might not know how to put three into twenty-one, but he's smart enough to know he don't want to be in hell-fire forever, so he says no. But then he asks Sullivan if it ain't wrong to tell a lie? And Brother Sullivan, he says telling a lie for God isn't a lie at all, so Weasel shouldn't worry about it. But he do worry about it—all the time, specially at bedtime, when he gets pictures in his head of what hellfire must be like, with devil eyes staring outta it, right at him. Forever. It's so bad he can't fall asleep. So he lays awake thinking Brother Sullivan is coming to get him to go down to his office again. Which is how come he ended up in the closet, hidin'.

"Jesus, kid," says Mikey when he hears the story. "No wonder ya can't sleep. Listen, come on out and get back to yer bed, and let me keep an eye out for Sullivan tonight."

"What about the devil eyes?" says Weasel.

"I'll watch for them too," says Mikey.

Next day, Mikey gets a message to me for to come over to Cliffside and meet him round back, where the fence is after falling down. Soon as I get there, he tells me Weasel's story.

"Jesus," I say. "Blackmail."

Mikey nods. "Gotta be. Tells the Brothers he's heard stories about 'em messing with the kids. Tell's 'em he got a witness. They pay up, he keeps it quiet—sends 'em away somewheres else. They don't, and him and his witness call the police."

"Wonder how much he squeezed outta them?" I say.

"How much can you get outta them Brothers?" Mikey asks. "They don't got much money."

"Their families does," I say. "Richest in St. John's, some of them. You bet they'd find a few thousand to keep their Mass-going son outta jail."

"So where d'ya figure he got it stashed?" asks Mikey. "A bank?"

"Too easy for the cops to track," I say. "Pro'bly got it hid in his apartment, behind a wall, or somewheres out in the country where nobody'd think to look. Me and thee'll have to have a look," I says, which we done—twice. Snuck into Sullivan's place, looked in every cupboard, under every pillow, opened every drawer except one, what were locked. I wanted to bust it open, but Mikey, he said no.

"If we crack it open," he says, "Sullivan'll know somebody's been pokin' round, and he'll move whatever's in there someplace we'll never find it. What we got to do is confront him, face to face, get it outta him that way."

"You figure he's just going to hand over the cash because we ask him to?"

"Some of it anyways," says Mikey. "We'll make a deal with him—split it with us, and we won't say nothing to the cops."

"And you figure the cops would believe us?"

"I figure Sullivan'd be worried they might—worried enough that he'd spend a few thousand to shut us up."

"And what if he ain't worried?" I say. "What if he tells us to go screw ourselves, to tell the cops whatever we wants, because there's no way they're gonna believe a couple of Sykeses?"

"Then I'd let you work on convincin' him," says Mikey.

"All right," I say.

Next weekend, we was ready. It were a Saturday night—movie night, when most of the boys and the Brothers were down to the common room. Sullivan, though, he stayed in his apartment, which is where he's to when we knocks on the door.

"Evening, Brother," says I, pushing my way inside, Mikey following behind. Mikey, he gets right to business, telling Sullivan we knows what he's up to. At first he tells us to go to hell—tells us the cops'll never believe a couple of ne'er-do-wells from Cook Street whose parents were crooked as a dog's hind leg. But Mikey, he gives him a few details of what we know—'bout how he got one of the kids to come down and say Brother so-and-so is diddlin' him, how one a the Brothers got so scared he keeled over on Sullivan's floor. Right away you can see Sullivan's rattled.

"We knows it all, b'y," I chimes in. "We even knows who the kid is. Who d'ya think told us all this, anyways?"

That rattles him good, I can tell, because he turns white as five pounds of flour. He's close to breaking, I knows it.

"Mikey," I says, "go out now and grab up that kid and bring him back here." Mikey looks like he don't want to go at first, but I gives him a hard look and says it again, slow.

"Go on, now, b'y. Shouldn't take you more'n five minutes to find him. Go on."

Soon as me and Sullivan is alone, I get to work, giving him a smack on the head, then another. I grabs his arm behind his back then and starts pulling up—the old cop move. He's weak—can't put up no fight, I can tell right away—so I push hard, feeling the arm starting to give.

"C'mon, you old bastard," I says. "Open the drawer you got locked."

He pulls out a key from his pants and unlocks it with his free arm. I slides it open but there's nothing there 'cept a black scribbler with a bunch of writing and numbers in it.

"What's this?" I say, shaking it in his face.

"It's nothing."

"So why's it locked in a drawer?"

I give his arm another yank and he starts crying.

"It's names," he says. "Names of Brothers I was blackmailing."

"And the numbers?"

"What they paid," he says.

"And where's the money to? Tell me or I'll break yer friggin' arm."

"It's not here—it's off out to the country."

"Show me," I says, flipping the scribbler to an open page. "Draw a map."

I lets go of his arm and it flops down like it's broke, but I can't tell if it is because I don't hear no snap. It don't matter—

it's his left arm, so the right one's still good, and that's the one he uses to draw the map.

"It's here," Sullivan says. "Out beyond Trepassey. There's a road, right here—a path—that runs out to the family chapel, built by the old ones when they first came over. It's abandoned, but part of it's still standing. There's a crypt underneath—my family's buried there. The money's there, in a cash box, in a coffin."

I looks at the map and sure enough, he's got a road drawed out and a path leading off it to the coast, but it ain't too clear on directions, I can see.

"Details," I says. "I needs to know exactly where it's to," and I gives him another slap and he starts writing underneath the drawing. Then he's finishes and looks up at me, still crying.

"Please," he says, "Please don't hurt me anymore."

And then...

Nick stops talking for a long while. The wind outside the car is strong now, moaning through the open window.

"Then you killed him," I say.

"I guess," says Nick, looking past me, out at the dust. "I guess—I don't remember much, just him begging me not to hurt him no more, and me thinking about all them little kids, and how they musta looked up at them grown men and begged the same thing, and how it didn't do them no good.

And something snapped—something I didn't even know was there to break."

"And my dad?"

"He never seen Sullivan after he left the room to get the kid. Once I knowed Sullivan were dead, I tore out the map from the scribbler, locked the apartment door from inside and took off out through the back window, off the fire escape. Twenty minutes later I was thumbing my way toward Trepassey."

"But you never found the money."

"Not for lack of trying. For three days I looked. Followed a dozen rabbits tracks from the road out to the coast, nothing at the end of any a them. Not a gravestone, not a pile of rocks, nothing."

"You think Sullivan was lying?"

"I wondered, but I don't know. He coulda been. But he were one scared bastard when he drawed out that map. He knew I'd come back for him if I didn't find nothing. Anyways, wherever it was I couldn't find a hint of it after three days' hard slog. And it were hard—nothing to eat but blueberries and only pond water to drink, so I had the shits by the second day. Come the third day I couldn't stand no more. I knowed I had to turn myself in or die in the country."

"That's when you mailed the letter," I say.

Nick nods. "Back to me old aunt Esther. Bit of a boozer, but smart enough to hold on to a map what comes in the mail."

"How'd my dad know she had it?"

"I told him," says Nick. "After I got arrested they hauled me back to St. John's, to the Pen. I had a visit or two with

Mikey—even Sykeses get visits with their family—and I told him to go by Aunt Ester's in a while, once all this had settled down, and she'd have something for him. Which he didn't want to hear. He was all panicked, with the murder and all, and didn't want to have anything to do with the map nor me nor anything else. 'That's fine,' I says. 'Just get it, put it in the safety deposit box.' The old man—Dick—had rented it out in Mikey's name."

"My dad had a safety deposit box?"

"Sure, we all did," says Nick. "The old man rented half a dozen, all across the island—places to stash stuff what he didn't want the cops to find. Anyways, I told Mikey to shove it in his box and forget about it till I got out. Then I'd get back in touch and we'd have a real good look without the cops breathing down our necks."

"But my dad, he testified against you."

Nick gives a smile. "Part of the plan. See, once my lawyer told me the prosecution had a witness what seen me leaving the room, I figured I were done for—they had me for killing Sullivan, no doubt. But they didn't have no motive, because as far as they knowed, I took nothing from the room—didn't rob him, didn't steal from him, nothing. So what would happen, I thought to myself, if I supplied the motive?"

"How do you mean?"

"Listen—they knows I killed Sullivan, right? But they don't know why. So they figure...what? I was trying to rob him, and maybe got scared? So that's murder—life sentence, at least twenty-five years in prison. But what if I tells them

Sullivan was trying it on with me, that he abused me? Then I could plead self-defence, saying I was only trying to protect myself. Except that would be a bit too obvious, right? The cops would figure I was just making up a story to save meself. But if Mikey told them I'd been abused—if he agreed to testify against me, saying I killed Sullivan because he assaulted me back when I were living at Cliffside—they might believe that. Mikey tells his story and all of a sudden I go from being some criminal kid who kills an innocent Brother to some poor orphan who were getting revenge for being abused at the hands of a pervert. And it worked, b'y. Five years, they give me, the jury practically crying at my story. And I'd a been out in four if it weren't for that bit of bother while I was inside."

Nick sits smoking for a long time before he says, "Now you knows."

"And what happens now?"

"Now," says Nick, "you gives me a hand, tracking this down."

He taps the map with his claw.

"But how can I help find anything? I don't even know where I am."

"You're young, you got fresh eyes. You could spot something I missed, see something I didn't when I were studying on that map. No question, you can help me out. Big time."

He starts the car up and moves back onto the highway.

"Once I find the stash, I'll drop you off somewhere on the way back to town, no harm done. But for now, you can help me find this place. The sooner that's done, the sooner you can be off with Dez or Frankie or that cute one what lives down the Gut."

The main road's nothing to see but rocks and rain. We drive for a long while with nobody talking. I look at my dad's watch; it's almost 4:00 PM. The rain's stopped, but it's still gray and dark, the sun shut up behind clouds that go as far as I can see. The road's swinging down close to the ocean more often now, and there's flecks of spray coming off the white waves. Once we see a little fishing boat, going up and down and sideways on the waves. A couple of cars go by, headed for town, and once a pickup passes us, with Nick telling me to lean down in the seat when he spots it coming in the rearview mirror. But that's all the cars we see. And that little boat.

"Here," says Nick after a while, passing me the map. "See that line marked *Number 10*? That's the road we're on now. Just coming up on Trepassey."

"I see it."

"Now," says Nick. He's looking between me and the road. "Just before Trepassey, that's where Sullivan drawed the path off from the main road. See the little line? He's got it branching off right by the church what he drawed in. But that's what I couldn't find. I mean, I found the church—it's right up here."

Nick slows the car down and turns off the road up toward a little white church. He drives in behind it, so you can't see the car from the highway, then shuts it off.

"See?" he says. "No trouble finding the church, but where's the path? I couldn't find nothing going off behind it—

leastways, nothing that led to no graveyard. What's he got written there, about where to look?"

I look at Sullivan's map. The writing's messy, scrawly, like mine would be if somebody just tried to snap my arm off. Some bits are so messy that they're crossed out and printed again, neater.

"Path starts behind church," I read.

"Right," says Nick. "I got that part."

"But it's not this church," I say. "See?"

I read the directions Sullivan wrote out twenty years ago. "Path runs behind St. Giles Anglican—just off Natches Road."

"Jesus Christ," says Nick. "Not this church?"

"Nope," I say, nodding at the sign in front of the church. "This is St. Mary's Catholic. We need to keep looking—to find that Natches Road."

"Christ," says Nick. "No wonder I couldn't find the right friggin' path."

He starts the car.

"You're pretty good with that reading," he says, once we're back on the main road.

"Guess so."

"That's good. That's good. Yer old man was like that too—always reading stuff, even went to the library. Bringing books home. That's good."

"Sign coming up," I say after a bit. It's a little green one, on a pole: *Natches Road*.

"This is it," I say.

Nick turns left onto it.

"See?" he says. "Good eyes. Me, I wouldn't a been able to read that till we was well down the road."

A couple secs later we're pulling into St. Giles's mud parking lot.

"Okay, Charlie," says Nick, parking behind the church. "Let's have a walk-round and see if we can spot that path. You okay on those crutches?"

"Pretty good."

"Good. Put that urn in your backpack. We'll take it along in case we bump into anybody—we can say we're out to scatter yer old man's ashes. No crime in that."

He opens the trunk and pulls his own pack outta the car.

"Church is tucked away in here pretty good," he says. "No wonder I couldn't find it back in '89."

"But it's just what Sullivan wrote," I say, unfolding the map to read the directions. "Path to crypt runs up from behind St. Giles...see?"

I hold the letter up for Nick to read. He doesn't bother looking, so I say it again.

"See?"

I point at the stuff Sullivan wrote about St. Giles. Nick studies it for a minute, then heads off toward the woods behind the church, turning left when he reaches the trees.

"Where you going?" I call out. "You turn right—he's got it written here—turn right behind the church. I just showed you. You just read it..."

Then I know—he didn't just read it, because he can't read. And right when I figure that out another bit of the truth slides into place, a little bit I don't really want to know, a little bit that makes me dizzy, pulls me back to the edge of that black hole.

Nick comes back toward me, telling me to hurry up.

"C'mon, Charlie, b'y. We're close—we just got to scout around a bit and find that path. Then we'll—"

"Nick," I butt in, serious—so serious that he stops talking. "You can't read, can you?"

He gives a laugh. "Funny time to be asking about readin'."

"But you can't, can you?"

The smile drops off his face.

"No. I can't. A few words. My address. And my aunt's. I knowed enough letters to write them out."

"But you can't read this writing," I say, holding up the map. "And you couldn't twenty years ago."

"No."

I'm falling now, into the hole, and I hear a voice echoing around in my head as I go. It's my own.

"It wasn't you." I hear what I say like I'm a different person, like I'm looking down at myself from somewhere up above, seeing how small I look. How stupid I am. How much I don't know. "It wasn't you who stayed alone with Sullivan, in that room, was it?"

We're both quiet, both waiting for that strange voice to come outta me again.

"It was my father, wasn't it?"

"Jesus, Charlie," says Nick. "Why don't you leave it, b'y? Leave it at what I told ya."

"Because it's not the truth, is it? About what happened."

"Listen to you," says Nick, "going on about the truth, and you all of eleven years old."

"I am not eleven," I shout. "I am thirteen. I been thirteen for seven months."

"So enjoy being thirteen for another eight months or whatever it is," says Nick, shouting right back. "Enjoy being thirteen and not knowing the truth about a few things. There's a lot to be said for not knowing the truth, specially when you're a kid—with all them nice things like Santa and the Easter Rabbit and all that other crap."

"I know there's no Santa Claus," I say. "And no Easter Rabbit and no Tooth Fairy and no elves out in the woods or wizards off in some other place I can't see. You think I believe in fairy tales? I can't even believe in a mom or a dad—all that stuff got torn away. But I gotta believe in something."

All of a sudden the anger just kind of drips outta me, like it's pouring outta my boots, and a heavy sadness I feel bending my shoulders seeps in to replace it.

"Do you know what I'm talking about, Nick? I know I'm thirteen, and you're forty-whatever you are. And I'm just some kid from out in Alberta, and you're a tough guy who lived in prison. But I hope you know what I'm talking about—how I gotta have something to believe. Something that's the truth. Something to stand my feet on."

After a long while he nods. "How'd you figure it out?"

"Because a this," I say, holding up the map. "If you could read, you never would have gone to that first church—you'd a kept going to Natches Road, like we did today."

"So I can't read. So what?"

"So whoever was in the room with Sullivan—whoever wanted him to put more details about where the money was—they could read."

"How'd ya figure that?"

"Because the map's the first thing Sullivan did—the first thing he put on the paper, at the top. But it wasn't good enough, so whoever was there wanted more details. And if that person was you, you wouldn't have got him to write out a bunch of directions you couldn't read. You'd a gotten him to draw more stuff on the map so you could figure out what he meant. But the person in Sullivan's room, they made him write it out. And when Sullivan's writing got too messy to read, they made him write it out again, neater. Which somebody who couldn't read would never do, because how could they tell if something made sense or not?"

Nick's smiling a sad smile, which he sticks a cigarette into.

"Your old man wanted it that way, you know," he says, putting his head down to light the smoke. He makes one of those old-man growls in his throat and shoots a big spit out onto some bushes.

"Wanted to be the tough guy on this one—do it all himself. 'It's my idea, and I'm doing it,' he says. Tired of me being in charge. So that's how we played—just like he wanted. He goes right into Sullivan's room, he gives him a poke or two to soften him up, he sends me off to look for Weasel."

"But you never brought Weasel back to the room," I say.

"Couldn't find him. He were probably off hiding some-wheres. So I had a smoke, stopped off for a piss and come back to Sullivan's room."

"And you went back in."

"And I went back in and found 'em—Sullivan on the floor, blood coming from his head and his mouth, yer dad standing over him, white as new sheets on the line."

"So my dad…he killed him."

"Just what I thought when I opened the door—said it too."

"Jesus, Mikey, what're ya after doing—giving him a crack on the head?"

"No, I gave him a smack or two," says Mikey, "but nothing too fierce," he says, holding up the map. "Just some encourage-ment to keep him going with the directions."

"When he were done," says Mikey, "he started to stand up, so I gives him a good shove to set him back down. He spun round and fell, smack into that table there."

I see the table plain enough: a low one, with a sharp edge Sullivan musta hit when he fell.

"And he ain't moved since?" I say.

"Nope," says Mikey. "But there's no way what I done was enough to kill him. Maybe he's just knocked out, or he's after having a heart attack or something."

I feel around his neck for a heartbeat, but there's nothing. No more blood pumping out either, which I know from the fights I been in is a bad sign.

"Well," I say, "it don't much matter what killed him. What matters is he's dead."

"Should we call somebody?" says Mikey. "The cops, the ambulance?"

"Sure, he's dead, b'y," I says. "What are the cops going to do except stick it on us? Screw that. We'll be in the lock-up five minutes after they gets here. No—better to leave him where he's to and let whoever finds him call it in."

"And that's just what we done, Mikey going out the door, me out the window. And it woulda a been fine, too, 'cept for that kid what seen me leaving."

"But after you were arrested," I say. "Why didn't you tell the police what happened?"

"What?" says Nick. "That we gone to Sullivan's room to grab the cash he got from blackmailing the Brothers? That'd look good in court."

"But you never killed him—you could prove it—that he banged his head or had a heart attack or something. They can do tests."

"Jesus, Charlie, you're watching too much TV, b'y. This weren't *CSI New York*. This were St. John's, 1989. Sure, the cops had their list of suspects all drawed up before they even arrived to a murder. All they had to do was find a bit of evidence to make it stick."

"But you still could have told them the truth—how it was my dad who was with Sullivan when he died."

"Could've," says Nick. "But then what woulda happened? They'd a banged Mikey around, pushed him about what he was really doing in Sullivan's room. And Mikey—no offence to your old man, Charlie—he woulda cracked. He woulda told

em everything, bout how we was putting the squeeze on
Sullivan, how he drawed the map out for us, where he told us
the money was to—everything woulda come out. And they still
wouldn't believed Mikey about not laying a hand on Sullivan.
Fact, they'd a figured he had it all planned out before he ever
went inside Sullivan's room, and having a plan makes it first-
degree murder—twenty-five years the hard way at Dorchester."

Nick lights another smoke off the first one.

"He wouldn't a lasted a month. Better for me to take the
blame—to get Mikey to make up some story what gives me the
motive, makes it look like I did it outta revenge. I gets the short
sentence, the map stays secret, and five years later when we're
still a couple of lads, we find the stash and live happily ever after."

"But what about what people thought?" I say. "How they
figured you were a killer?"

Nick gives a snort that builds up into a long belly laugh.

"What people thought?" he says when the laugh finally
turns to a cough. "About me?"

He flicks the smoke away and comes close enough to lay
his good hand on my shoulder.

"What they thought was that I were murdering, evil
Cook Street scum, soon as they heard the cops was looking
for me. And even if I had the best lawyer in town, and even
if he got me off. And even if the judge stood on them stone
steps to the courthouse on Water Street and called out for
all the town to hear—called out to all them reporters and
gawkers and do-gooders—that I were an innocent man.
Even if all that happened, people still woulda thought I was

a murdering, evil Cook Street scum who was lucky enough to get away with it."

I look at his eyes; they're angry, but not at me.

"It just seems like…I don't know…it seems like a lot to pay for something you didn't do," I say.

"I didn't just pay, Charlie."

"Twenty years locked up seems like paying to me."

"But I got something out of it too. I got to do right by my brother, which I wanted to do, because he were the smart one in the family, the good one. Like with Weasel. When I heard his story, all I thought of was the money and how to get it. But yer old man, he were mad—it got him angry, what them Brothers was doing. Don't get me wrong, Mikey weren't no saint. He wanted the money too. But he wanted something more. Something like…I don't know…justice, I'd guess you'd call, though neither the pair of us woulda used that word. But I think that's what he wanted when he gave Sullivan that last shove, the one that sent him to the floor. A bit of justice for all them little kids what never had a chance to fight back. And even me, stupid as I was back then, even I knowed that was something worth having—that feeling that ya should stand up for something, that ya should find a way to do some good. Growing up, I never felt it meself—not when I was beating on some kid who owed me money, or when I was trying to feel up some girl I took a liking to. I always just took what I wanted, not a thought about anybody else."

"Except for my dad."

"Except for yer dad," says Nick. "And it felt good, doing right by him. That's what I mean about me not just paying—that I got something too. I got to stand up for my blood, to help somebody what might be able to do a bit of good in the world, 'stead of harm."

Nick looks at me for a bit.

"But I don't know if that's something you could understand, you being a thirteen-year-old from Alberta, and me being forty-whatever I am and a tough old bastard who spent years locked up."

I take a look behind him. The sun is out from behind the clouds now. It's just starting to go down, turning the green hill gold.

"I figure it is," I say, swinging my crutches toward the hill. "Guess we better find the path before it gets too dark."

TWENTY-TWO

It's not much of a path when we find it, just a steep brown squiggle running up through the little trees.

"Tuckamore," Nick says, giving them a kick. "Don't look like much, but it's tough—lives for hundreds of years on not much more'n fog and salt air. Wind blows so hard out here most of the time it can't grow up straight because it gets blowed over. So it grows sideways, along the ground."

I see what he means about the wind when we get higher. It's like walking toward a giant fan that never shuts off. It slows me down, because I have to bend into it. With my cast dragging along, it takes us close to an hour to get to the top, but we finally crest the hill and in front of us is ocean, blue and white and green and black all the way to where it touches the sky. Bigger than anything I've ever seen, a million tiny mountains moving like one giant muscle. Behind us there's the tuckamore that ends at the cliff. And below the cliff, sixty meters down, there's a line of white foam running down the coast on either side where the waves hit the rock. I hear them rolling in, *boom, boom, boom.*

"Got a blow comin'," says Nick, looking out at the white-caps. I expect to see him frowning, but he's got a big smile on.

"I dreamed about this," he says, looking out to sea. "Night after night after night. I dreamed about this."

"About the wind?"

"The wind." He nods. "There's no wind in prison. Ever. Just pissy little breezes, carrying someone else's stink. Not even out in the yard, when a gale blows. The big brick wall— it breaks it up 'fore it can find your face."

He stands still for a long time, breathing in and out. I watch his cigarette burn down in his claw, glowing in the wind. It burns to ash, and still he keeps looking out at the sea.

"I'll not go back inside," he says at last. "I'll do no more time sitting in stink, counting days."

He remembers the cigarette and goes to flick it, but it's burned itself out, the ashes gray in his fingers. He brushes them off and turns to me. His eyes are glistening—tearing up in the breeze—and he gives them a wipe with a finger so black I think it'll leave a stain on his cheek.

"Now you see why that tuckamore grows like it do," he says, wiping the other eye before he turns to the ocean again. He says something else, something about the mainland, but I can't hear.

"What?" I say, reaching out to tug his jacket.

"Nothing," he says. "Nothing. Now, what's Brother Sullivan tell us to do next?"

I read, "Turn right at the top of the hill and follow the path another hundred yards. Foundation stones to old chapel are on right, fifty feet back from cliff. Family crypt is underneath, through cellar door."

"Let's go," says Nick. He gives a nod over his shoulder at the sun. "Light'll be gone soon."

The foundation is right where the letter says, a stone square of rocks on the ground with a rotten old roof on top. Off to one side there's a busted-up wooden door set in the stones—I guess the only way down into the crypt. Nick walks over to it and sets down his backpack, pulling out a flashlight and a pry bar.

"This is it, Charlie, b'y," he says. The smile leaves his face as he clicks on the light. "Do the letter say anything about where to look once we're down there?"

I read the last paragraph, "Go down steps—cash box is in coffin closest to door."

Nick takes a deep breath and looks at me. "Coming?"

"As far as the door. Then I'll keep watch."

"Fair enough," says Nick, pushing on the door. There's a creak when it opens; then he's inside, the flashlight pointed down the steps. He swings a hand in front of his face, brushing off cobwebs that run from the doorway up to the wooden beams on the ceiling. He moves farther down, and I stick my head in far enough to see where he goes. It smells old and moldy, like cardboard boxes going black in a basement. Where the light shines I see rough stones and moss, water sparkling when the beam catches it dripping. Everywhere else is black. Nick takes a last step and he's onto a mud floor.

"This one," he says, pointing the light at the wooden box closest to him. It's stained dark, I can tell, and it's smaller than I expected. Not a coffin, really—just a long, thin box.

"Probably," I say. "Closest to the door."

He stands at the coffin, working the pry bar under the lid. He gives a grunt and there's a ripping sound—a screw yanking outta wood. He moves the bar along the edge and pries up another bit and another till finally the whole thing pops off onto the mud floor.

"Charlie," he calls. I don't move, so he calls again.

"C'mon, b'y. There's nothing down here what's going to do you no harm. C'mon now and grab hold a this light."

I step down onto the floor and take it.

"There's another box in here—a little 'un," he says. "Give us some light while I gets it out."

Nick reaches down and grabs the smaller box, stirring up dust when he picks it up.

"Now," he says, cradling it in his arm. "How do you figure you opens this?"

I take a closer look.

"It's not a cash box," I say. "It's an urn—like for my dad's ashes."

"Well," says Nick, "it's plenty big to hide a good bit of cash. C'mon, let's get it open."

"Here," I say, reaching for the box. "On my dad's there's a button you press."

Nick's finger finds mine in the gloom and brushes it aside as he presses the button. A second later the lid swings open. He shoots his claw deep inside, swirling dust as he moves it back and forth.

"Shhhit," he says, teeth tight together. "Nothing but goddamn ashes."

He snarls, pulling his hand out, streaked black and gray in the flashlight beam.

"The old lying bastard," he says, dropping the urn back into the box. "The lying bastard."

"Maybe not," I say. I reach past Nick and pick up the urn. "I mean, Sullivan—he was alive when he wrote the letter," I say.

"Jesus, Charlie," Nick says. "It ain't the time to be arsing around. Course he were alive."

"I'm not kidding around," I say, brushing dust off the urn with my sleeve. There's a brass plate on the lid, covered in twenty years of dirt.

"Maybe we're not looking for the coffin you just opened," I say. I point to another coffin, the one right behind Nick, farther from the door, with a wooden lid split open with age. "Maybe we're looking for that one."

"How'd you figure?"

"Because when Sullivan drew the map, that older box *was* the one closest to the door. But then Sullivan died…"

Nick gives his forehead a smack.

"And he got buried here too," he says.

I brush off the brass engraving and read, "Sean Seamus Sullivan: 1935 to 1989. *Cineres cineribus, pulverem pulveri.* I don't know what that last bit means."

"It means," says Nick, "that these here is Sullivan's ashes— he were the last one what got put in."

He turns to the old coffin next to Sullivan's box and rips off the lid, shining the beam into it.

"Take this," he says, passing the light to me. There's bones inside, and a skull, down at one end, a big crack in it like someone smashed it open a couple hundred years ago. Pro'bly with some old ax. I woulda figured bones'd be white, like in the movies, but these are gray and fuzzy with dust, halfway to ashes.

Nick sends all that stuff flying when he reaches in and jumbles his hand round in the bones.

"Got it," he says, pushing some leg bones off a box that's hidden below.

It's black, hard, steel. Nick's eyes are wide.

"It's the cash box," he says. "It's heavy."

He swings it off the coffin and down onto the mud floor.

"The light. Down here."

He's got the pry bar on it, trying to work it under the edge. There's sweat dropping off his nose as he twists it, looking for a crack. All of a sudden he raises the bar up and smacks the box, again and again, till finally there's a bulge in the lip where he shoves the bar. He gives one last giant pull and the lid pops open. Coins—lots of them—spill into a pool of yellow onto the mud floor.

"Loonies," I say.

"These ain't loonies," says Nick, picking one up. "There's writing on them."

He passes one to me. "What's it say?"

"It's not a word I know—I'm not sure how to say it."

"Well, what's it sound like?"

"It's like, Kreeger, Kruger…"

"Krugerrand," says Nick.

"Guess so…yeah. Krugerrand."

"I never seen 'em before," says Nick, "but I heard of 'em plenty, specially during my last stretch doing soft time in minimum. Some of the white-collar crowd—the business boys what done a fraud—they hid some of their money by buying these up. Can't trace 'em, easy to smuggle in and outta places. It's gold."

"Gold coins. What're they worth?"

"I don't got a clue, but they got to be worth a fair bit. A guy could smuggle one a these into the Pen and get six months of easy living outta it."

"Easy living?"

"Sure. Slip it to a guard and you got yourself extra food, good yard work, drugs, booze. Whatever you wants."

"But we're not in prison."

"Don't matter, b'y. This is cash, Charlie—cash dollars. Thousands of 'em. Tens of thousands, maybe. Here. Help me collect 'em."

We toss them into a pile, brush them off a bit, drop them back into the cash box and head for the steps, Nick in front.

"Keep that light on the steps, now," he says, walking slow. "I don't want to tumble and spill this bunch."

I'm just stepping out onto the ground when the world goes white, the beam from a big flashlight right in my eyes, a gruff voice coming outta the glare.

"Take another step," it says, "and I'll put a bullet in each a ya."

TWENTY-THREE

"Whoa," says Nick, holding the box in one hand, shielding his eyes with the other. "No need to be adding holes to nobody, me old son. Who am I talking to anyways?"

"Never mind," says the voice. It's coming from the path, out where it runs along the edge of the cliff. The full moon's out now, behind the voice, so there's just a silhouette, with the sea sprawling out behind.

"What are you two doing up here?" he says.

"Me and the nephew was just out for a hike and stayed a bit too long admiring the view—got caught out in the dark. We're from town, see, and I weren't sure if we should try heading back to the car or camp out here for the night. That's why we was checking out the old chapel—seeing if there was a spot to lay our heads."

"You don't need to worry about where you'll sleep," says the voice. I recognize it now.

"It's Tubby," I whisper.

"Tubby?" Nick whispers back.

"The cop. The one keeping an eye on me."

"A townie cop?" Nick says, and for the first time since I met him there's something in his voice—a little rise, a little tremble, like a river going over rocks—something scared. "What's a townie cop doing out here?"

"You two," Tubby shouts. "No talking."

Nick turns back to the glare. "The nephew here, he were just telling me he thinks he knows ya. Says you're a cop what's been keeping an eye on him in town."

There's no answer, just the glare.

"You're a bit off your patch, ain't cha?'" says Nick. "This is Mountie territory, I figure."

"You'd know, wouldn't ya, Sykes," says Tubby. "It was Mounties chasing you round this hill twenty years ago."

"It were."

Nick's nervous, the claw clicking open and shut in the white light.

"So ya got any Mounties with ya, Constable?"

"It's Sergeant," comes the voice. "And no, I don't got any Mounties with me. It's just me and thee. And this."

Tubby taps metal against metal, then shows the barrel of a pistol in the flashlight beam.

Nick nods. "I heard they give you guys guns a few years back. Ever shoot yours?"

"Just at the range," says Tubby. "So far."

"Maybe it don't work," says Nick. He looks back at me and gives a wink.

Right when he turns back to Tubby there's a boom, and a flash comes from the end of the gun—a devil's tongue licking the night. I grab my ears, it's so loud, and drop my flashlight into the tuckamore, the beam pointing right at Tubby. He's smiling, smoke from the barrel coming at me on the wind, smelling like a thousand cap guns gone off at once, burning my nose, metal in my mouth. Tubby points his flashlight at the wood door behind us, the one we just came out of; it's got a hole big as my head blown in it, splinters all white and jagged.

"It works," he says in a shout, all our ears ringing.

Then all of a sudden my guts are water and a cramp bends me double.

"I gotta go," I say.

"Go?" says Tubby. "You ain't going nowhere."

"No," I say, "I mean…I gotta go, right now."

"So go," Tubby says. "Right there. I'll even give ya a bit of privacy."

He moves the light over onto Nick, so I'm in the dark when I drop my pants.

"You okay?" calls Nick after a minute. He looks at Tubby. "I'm just going to see if the kid's okay—don't shoot or nothing."

"Go ahead," says Tubby. "You Sykeses are used to getting one another out of all sorts of shit."

I stand up and fasten up my jeans as Nick comes over. He puts his hand on my shoulder.

"That happens sometimes," he says, "even if nobody don't ever talk about it. Nothing to feel bad about. You okay?"

I nod.

He leans in to whisper in my ear, "Charlie, listen. We got trouble here—whoever this guy is, he's half friggin' nuts. We got no choice but to try and get ourselfs outta here, so I wants you to follow me—slow. Toward the path."

He straightens up and takes a step toward Tubby, with me behind. A few more steps and we're almost at the cliff edge and the path. I hear the waves riding in. *Boom, boom, boom.*

"Stop. Right. There," Tubby says, blocking the path with the sea at his back. There's a metal-on-metal *clink* again, and I can see his badge and a gun barrel glint in the moonlight. It's pointed right at Nick's chest.

"Take another step and you'll be dead in the dirt, Sykes," he says.

"All right, b'y," says Nick, holding up his hands. "Relax—no need to be pointin' that thing at the kid and me. Wouldn't want it to go off accidental."

"It won't be an accident when it goes off," says Tubby.

"When?" says Nick. He tries to give a little laugh, but it comes out dry and chopped up. "Whaddaya mean 'when'?" The ripple's back in his voice.

"I mean when you try to make a run for it," says Tubby. He gives a low laugh, slow and deep. "You know, when you see me coming over the hill to rescue the kid you kidnapped. That's when you make a run for it, see? Tragic that the kid gets caught in the cross fire. But that's what happens when you're dealing with a crazed killer on the run."

"But I ain't tryin' to run nowheres," says Nick. "I ain't got nothin' to escape from—like I told ya, me and the kid, we was just out for a walk, scattering a few of his old man's ashes out here by the ocean."

"Cut the crap, Sykes," says Tubby. "I know what you're doing out here."

Nick gives a shrug. "And what's that?"

"You're looking for Sullivan's money," says Tubby. He raises the beam so it hits the cash box. "And I'd say you found it."

Nick looks over at me and gives me a quick shake of his head.

"You remember Sullivan, don't ya, Sykes? How you killed him? How you split his head open?"

Boom, boom, boom comes up from the rocks.

"I remember him too," says Tubby. "Proper thing—him being my first murder."

"You worked that case?" says Nick. "You was barely off your mother's tit back in '89. What was you…eighteen?"

"Twenty," says Tubby. "Old enough to be stuck working a Saturday night, riding a radio car up and down George Street looking for drunks. That's what I was doing when the call came in—body found, Cliffside."

"You was working that night," says Nick.

"I was," says Tubby. "Couldn't believe it when the call came in. Didn't know it was murder right off—just a body. Coulda been a heart attack, seizure, OD. But it was a chance to hit the lights and tear on up to Cliffside, which I done in under two minutes. Soon as I came through the door I knew I had something serious—the blood, the old boy's head busted in. I called the detectives, taped off the door and waited. And while I was waiting I had a bit of a look round, to see if I could impress the suits with a bit of evidence when they showed. That's how I come to find this."

Tubby pulls something from his pocket, black and shiny in the flashlight beam.

"Jesus," Nick whispers.

"Recognize it, do ya, Sykes?" says Tubby. "I don't doubt ya do, since you were the last one but me to lay hands on it—when you tore out that page. The one with the map."

Nick shoots me another look, with another head shake.

"Made for interesting reading," says Tubby, "all those numbers, all those names. Tied in with some rumors we'd been hearing at the station, 'bout how Brothers was paying somebody to get transferred outta the province. Then I come to find this notebook, the last thing the dead man bothered to write in."

"And you took it," says Nick.

Tubby nods, the badge on his cap bouncing moonbeams back.

"I took it. Slipped it off that desk and into my pocket and took it home to have a closer look—at my leisure, like. The first thing I see is a page is ripped out. Then I see that right under that, there's something faint, like a drawing. A map. Too faint to see where's it's to, but a map. So I think to myself, What kind of a map is a dead man going to draw, a dead man who's a blackmailer? What kind of map is he going to draw just before he becomes a dead man?"

"You're a real Colombo," says Nick, whatever that means. Whatever it means, Tubby laughs at it.

"No," says Tubby, "Colombo was a lieutenant; I was just a rookie constable. But I was smart enough to know what that map was to, and smart enough to know you musta had it when we were out chasing you for those three days. Once you were picked up, I figured it'd all come out—the Mounties' would either find you with the money and start asking how you got it, or they'd find you with the map and start asking what it was to. But no   it didn't happen. You didn't have no money, and no map. Then your brother comes up with this story about how you hated Sullivan for abusing you, about how you were getting revenge, with never a mention of blackmail, never a mention of a map. And I knew—knew you two were cooking something up, planning how to do as little time as possible; then you'd hook up in a few years and grab the cash. So I waited to see what would happen when you got out—where'd you'd go. Because I figured the first place you'd go would be for the cash."

"And you planned on being right there behind me," says Nick.

Tubby laughs. "I did. What I didn't plan on was it being such a long wait. I mean, after you got manslaughter I figured you'd be out in five years, maybe less. But then you went and killed that guy in the Pen, and five jumped up to fifteen."

"I never killed nobody in the Pen."

"Court said otherwise, didn't it?" says Tubby. "Says you set that fire what killed the other inmate…"

"I never meant for nobody to die in that."

"Poor Nick Sykes. Never meant for anything to happen. I don't suppose you meant to kill Sullivan, either, did ya?"

"I never did," says Nick, his voice going to a shout. "I never…"

He looks over at me.

"I never meant to kill anyone."

"Well," says Tubby, "whether you meant to or not, you done the time—or most of it. Though I thought you had a couple more years to go…"

"Got out early for good behavior," says Nick.

"Guess that's why I got caught off-guard there, the night of the accident. I never figured you one for good behavior. Anyways, I was thinking I wouldn't have to worry about the Sykeses for another couple of years when all of a sudden there's that accident. My jaw just about hit the floor when the kid said his name, then his old man's. Jesus, I thought, something's up. Then I come to find out you been released, and it all came together: Mikey coming here, meeting you, heading off to wherever the cash was hid. So I kept close to the kid, figured he'd lead me to you, and you'd lead me to the cash, which is"— Tubby nods at the cash box—"in there."

"So today in town," says Nick, "you let me grab up Charlie."

Tubby smiles. "Had to. I knew you needed something from the kid, else you would've gone to where the cash was to and then took off. But you were hanging around, following him—to the funeral home, up on Signal Hill, out to Quidi Vidi. You wanted him for something, so I figured the sooner I let you get him, the quicker you'd lead me to the loot."

"And you tailed us here."

"Wasn't hard," says Tubby. "Seen you pull off into the gravel pit, then off down Natches Road, and on out to here. And this is where it ends, Sykes. Right here. Now give me the box."

"If I don't?" says Nick. "You'll what? Shoot me? You already said that's gonna happen—you're gonna shoot me and come up with some story bout how I were dangling Charlie off the cliff. So why don't I save you the trouble and take a jump right now and end it? Over the edge. With this lot going over with me."

Nick holds the box up as he edges toward the cliff, forcing Tubby to take a step backward.

"That's far enough now," says Tubby, shooting a quick glance behind him to see where the edge is. "Just give me the box, and I'll let the kid go."

Nick laughs. "You'll let him go…now why would I believe that?"

"I give you my word."

"Yer word?" says Nick. He spits. "What's yer word worth? Didn't ya already take some kind of oath to help out them what needs it? And here ya are, getting ready to gun me down in cold blood and toss me nephew off the cliff behind me. You're about as good at upholding the law as yer buddies were twenty years ago, when ye all turned yer blue backs on them kids at Cliffside. Christ, yer as bad as the Brothers. So go on, give me yer word, b'y. Shout it loud enough to knock the ears off a rabbit—it ain't worth nothing. Because I knows what you're gonna do, sure as shit. Soon as ya gun me down, you're gonna do the same to Charlie there. Then dump us both off the cliff. No doubt you got yer story cooked up already, 'bout how the kid got caught in the cross fire. That's how it's going to go down, ain't it, officer? I knows it. I can see it in you, you twisted prick."

And he can—I know it, just by looking at his eyes, glinting in the glare of the flashlight. Nick's got them drilling full-on, right into Tubby, and he sees just what's gonna happen. Tubby sees it too, and he takes a nervous half-step back, keeping himself and that gun barrel just outta Nick's reach.

"Believe me or not, Sykes," says Tubby. "I don't see you got much choice."

"Oh, I got a choice," Nick yells, then turns to me. "Charlie," he shouts. "You do better than I would have, all right? Do better for your dad, b'y. And for yourself. And for me. You do better with this."

Right when he says it, he tosses that cash box straight toward me, then puts his head down and his shoulders forward and runs hard as he can into Tubby and…they're gone. Gone like your room when the light goes out.

And it's just me and the moon and the *boom, boom, boom*, up from sixty meters below.

TWENTY-FOUR

I never saw what made my dad like he was—leastways, I never saw it till Nick told me the truth about what happened. About how my grandparents died, and about the orphanage and about what happened there. It explained a lot of things, hearing that. Explained how come my dad could seem mad sometimes, at nothing. How he got sad when he was drunk, sad at stuff I couldn't see. In fact, most of the times when he got mad or sad, it was at things I couldn't see—at ghosts almost. Which, I guess, is kind of what he was mad and sad about. His mom and his dad and those Brothers and the little kids. All that stuff happened a long time ago. But inside his head it was still right there, as real to him as last night's hockey score.

You'd think it would make me sad to find out about all that stuff, but you know what? It makes me happy. Well, not happy. But it makes me feel a bit better. I'll tell you a secret about those times when my dad got mad or sad at stuff I couldn't see. Deep down, I always figured it was because of me—because of something bad I did. For a long time, I couldn't figure out what it might be, that something bad. Then one afternoon, when I was four or five—before I started school—I figured it out. I remember the exact time, because me and my dad were at McDonald's. I was sitting at the table while he got our stuff, and I was looking at this little family across the aisle: a baby in a highchair and kid a bit older than me, keeping an eye on that baby to make sure it didn't flop out onto the floor. And while I was waiting for my dad, along comes those kids' mom with her tray. And she puts it down and passes out the fries and the ketchup and the straw and the napkins. And right then, watching her open up one of those stupid ketchup packets that spurt the goop everywheres, right then I figured it out: my dad hated me for killing my mom. Not that he hated me all the time...But those times when he got mad for no reason? Now I knew the reason. And the worst part was there was nothing I could do to make it better, 'cause even a five-year-old knows you can't bring someone alive who's been dead all that time.

That was the first time I got the feeling of that black hole trying to suck me into it—that day at McDonald's. Pretty soon after that I started having dreams that my mom wasn't really dead, that she might be out there somewheres, looking for me. And that was about the only thing that could make the black-hole feeling go away. Until today—until right now, when I think about what Nick told me. What Nick told me makes me figure maybe I wasn't the only reason my dad was like he was.

Maybe my mom dying was still part of it, but it wasn't just me. It wasn't just my fault. And that makes things a bit better.

Maybe that's part of what the truth does—makes things a bit better, even if it hurts finding out about some things.

That's what I'm thinking about, up on the cliff, with the last of the clouds blowing away, leaving a clear view of the stars—thousands of them, with the full moon off to one side. It's almost bright as day, bright enough to see if I can spot anything over the cliff. I haven't dared look since Nick charged into Tubby, but now I figure I gotta. I get down on my belly and slink out to the edge, poke my head out beyond the last of the rocks and the grass and the stones, and I look down.

There's only the ocean and the rocks where the waves hit the cliff. Nothing else. When I slink back from the edge, my cast bumps into my backpack, sitting where I set it before Nick headed down into the crypt. There's a sweatshirt in it that I get out, because it's cold with the sun gone down. And the urn's in there too.

Maybe this would be a good place to scatter those ashes, I think—with Nick close by somewheres. So I pull out the urn and creep back to the cliff edge, where I pop the top and turn it upside down. Nothing happens. I shake it, and still nothing happens. The ashes are stuck. How can something that's nothing get stuck to itself? But it does. I have to bash the bottom like a ketchup bottle to make the ashes fall out, and when they finally do, they come out in a clump before the wind catches them and explodes them a thousand ways:

up onto the tuckamore, out into the sea air, down onto the waves and the rocks and the cliff, silver dust in the moonlight.

My dad would like that, I bet—that wind blowing him around. I bet if he could pick a way to disappear, to really disappear so nobody'd ever find a trace of him again, that might be it. Into the wind on a cliff over the ocean in Newfoundland.

It's when I set the empty urn down that I get the idea of what I can do with those coins. I get the cash box that's lying in the tuckamore where Nick chucked it and set it down by the urn. They're almost the same size—it'd only take a second to move the coins from one to the other. Then I could just shut it up and take it back into town and put those coins right into that safety deposit box.

I open the cash box and count them—fifty-seven, which I don't know how much that is in dollars, but must be a lot. Enough to buy a bike, or a car even, when I'm old enough to drive. Or enough to get a ticket back out to Fort Mac when I decide I want to go. Then there'd still be some left over to build a camp, like the one me and Robert started down behind his place. Except we didn't have money to buy any real lumber or anything, so we just used up some of his dad's old plywood. I could maybe live there for a bit—till I was sixteen or something. Then I could rent a place or get a job or go to college. It'd be easy with this money.

Except...

It would mean telling lies, which is something I've already done plenty of, I guess. What's a few more? I already told

Dez and Miz I didn't know anything about why we came out here—that it was just a vacation. It'd be easy to keep on telling that lie. How I didn't know anything about what Nick wanted, or why Tubby ended up on the cliff. They might ask a couple of questions, but then they'd figure I was just what I was pretending to be: a dumb kid who didn't know about anything much.

But I'd know. And then I'd be like my dad, with all those ghosts in my head I couldn't talk to anybody about. I'd have to keep them all secret, for the rest of my life. And right now, what I want to do more than anything is to talk to somebody about this—even if they won't know exactly what to do. Just to talk to someone and maybe ask them what they think'd be best to do.

That's when I remember Clare's phone, still in my pocket. The sky over my head is going from deep black to dark blue when I start scrolling down the numbers to find the one I want.

It rings once.

"Hey," I say. "It's Charlie. Can you come get me?"

ACKNOWLEDGMENTS

Though the events in *Charlie's Key* are fictional, there were many, many real young boys who suffered physical and sexual assaults at the Mount Cashel Orphanage in St. John's, Newfoundland. It was widespread, horrific abuse that went unpunished for many years, ignored and covered up by both church and civic authorities. Michael Harris has written an excellent overview of their story in *Unholy Orders* (Viking Canada).

ROB MILLS has been an award-winning reporter, newspaper editor and writer in Nova Scotia, Newfoundland and Ontario. *Charlie's Key* is his first published novel. He lives in Peterborough, Ontario, with his wife and two daughters.